THE FAR HORIZON

THE FAR HORIZON

Basil Copper

Chivers Press ● G.K. Hall & Co.
Bath, England   Thorndike, Maine USA

This Large Print edition is published by Chivers Press, England, and by G.K. Hall & Co., USA.

Published in 2001 in the U.K. by arrangement with the author.

Published in 2001 in the U.S. by arrangement with Basil Copper.

U.K. Hardcover   ISBN 0-7540-4399-1   (Chivers Large Print)
U.K. Softcover   ISBN 0-7540-4400-9   (Camden Large Print)
U.S. Softcover   ISBN 0-7838-9327-2   (Nightingale Series Edition)

The text of this Large Print edition is unabridged.
Other aspects of the book may vary from the original edition.

Set in 16 pt. New Times Roman.

Printed in Great Britain on acid-free paper.

British Library Cataloguing in Publication Data available

Library of Congress Cataloging-in-Publication Data

Copper, Basil.
    The far horizon / Basil Copper.
        p.   cm.
    ISBN 0-7838-9327-2 (lg. print : sc : alk. paper)
    1. Faraday, Mike (Fictitious character)—Fiction 2. Private investigators—California—Los Angeles—Fiction. 3. Los Angeles (Calif.)—Fiction. 4. Large type books.   I. Title.
PR6053.O658 F37   2001
823'.914—dc21   00–047177

CHAPTER ONE

1

The rain was drumming nicely down the collar of my trenchcoat as I got out the Buick, slammed the door and walked up the wet zig-zag of crazy paving leading to the old Zangwill place. Old man Zangwill had phoned in earlier in the day pleading great urgency but as I'd been off the other side of town on stake-out I hadn't got the message until half an hour ago.

Stella had taken it, like always and she'd managed to calm the old boy. He was pretty upset according to her so I'd put my toe down all the way across town and up into the foothills where Zangwill lived. I'd made pretty good time considering the traffic and the weather conditions and it was still only early afternoon though you'd never have guessed it with the darkness of the sky.

It's like that sometimes in Southern California and the Pacific had looked sullen and stormy all the way out as I tooled along the beach road and then snaked up into the hills. I was damp and hungry now because I'd missed lunch in getting out here and I hoped the old man would offer me one of his dainty afternoon teas.

I understood he still kept a pretty fancy

establishment, even though the place was a little rundown these days. He even kept an English butler one time and gave great parties in the thirties but all that was gone now.

Stella had heard he still kept maids of an older generation who wore aprons and lots of lace on their uniforms. It sounded like one of those screwy old Hollywood pre-war movies to me but I'd come on out anyway. I'm like that. Good natured and generous-hearted. I grinned to myself and closed my raincoat collar against the driving shards of water as I put my size nines over the concrete. You're a great Christian martyr, Mike, I told myself.

I skirted a flowering hedge that was being spoiled by the climate right now and walked across a circular red gravel concourse toward a big flight of steps that led up to the Palladian portico. I would have driven up except that there had been iron chains locked across both ends of the circular drive so I had to go through the small white wicket gate set in the hedge in the middle of the property. I guessed it was one way old man Zangwill guarded his privacy. It was all right if you liked privacy but it was hard on the visitors.

There was a snarling noise coming from somewhere now. I stopped in my tracks, moved over and got back into the shelter of the hedge. The noise was coming from the other side and it sent faint vibrations up and down my spine. I didn't have to look to know what it was. It was a guard-dog loose in the grounds; probably a Dobermann Pinscher by the sound of it. I knew the noise an Alsatian makes.

The Dobermann and the Alsatian are the two principal breeds used for guard purposes and by professional security companies, so it had to be the former. I worked my way up cautiously to the end of the hedge. I was getting nice and damp by this time. The big black dog bounded out suddenly, making no noise except for the faint clicking of its claws on the gravel. Its deep red eyes glowed smokily and there was a murmuring vibration back in its throat.

I stayed where I was, bringing up my right forearm. If the worst came to the worst I could jam it in its throat. There was a low, throaty chuckle from behind the hedge and a big man in a wide-brimmed hat, whose dark slicker was streaming with water looked at me approvingly.

'Excellent, mister. You done just what I would have done.'

'I'm glad I got something right,' I said, lowering my arm.

The big man, who had security guard written all over him, showed me square yellow teeth. He lowered the double-barrelled shotgun under his arm so that it was pointing at the gravel.

'All right, Satan,' he said to the dog.

The big Dobermann melted back behind the hedge again.

'You've got him well-trained,' I said.

The man in the slicker gave me another sixteen millimetres worth of smile.

'He could have torn your throat out before you'd have known it. You got business here?'

I nodded.

'Mr Zangwill sent for me. My name's Faraday.'

The big man nodded, his face clearing.

'I'll have to ask for your identification.'

'Sure,' I said.

I got out the photostat of my licence in the plastic holder and showed it to him. He took it and wrinkled up his face like he was having difficulty deciphering its contents. He grunted and handed it back to me.

'My name's Kempton, Mr Faraday. Sorry about all the melodrama but Mr Zangwill keeps tight security up here.'

'You can say that again,' I said.

I put the photostat back in my billfold and put that in my pocket. I re-buttoned my raincoat.

'Anything that says we have to stand here getting wet?' I said.

Kempton shrugged, a slow smile breaking out on his lean, leathery features.

'Hell, no. It is rather humid now that you come to mention it. I'll walk you to the porch. It's only a few yards. Miss Billington will be

4

anxious to see you.'

'Who might she be?' I said.

He moved ahead of me, holding the shotgun carelessly under his arm.

'She's the old man's secretary. He won't do a thing without her.'

'Nice is she?' I said.

He shot me a shrewd glance through the falling shroud of rain.

'If you like them like that, Mr Faraday. Too young for me. But then you're a much younger man.'

'Kind of you to say so,' I said.

He stopped suddenly as we were going up the front steps, like something had occurred to him.

'You carry a gun, Mr Faraday?'

'Sometimes on cases,' I said. 'Not today.'

He nodded and led the way ahead again.

'That's all right then. Because if you had I'd have to take it off you.'

I grinned.

'You just going to take my word for it?'

He nodded solemnly, glancing back over his shoulder.

'Sure. You've got an honest face. Besides, I figure you're clean. I brushed against you coming up the steps and I couldn't feel a thing.'

'Why did you ask me then?' I said.

Kempton gave me a twisted smile.

'Just force of habit. Besides, this is one of

the most boring jobs I've ever had.'

We were in the shadow of the porch now and once we got in underneath out the rain I shook my coat and sponged my face with my handkerchief.

'What's Zangwill afraid of?' I said.

Kempton looked at me shrewdly, shifting from one big foot to the other. His eyes were suddenly hard and suspicious. There was no sign of the dog but I knew it wouldn't be far off. He probably had one of those special whistles that could summon it in a second.

'I'd rather him tell you that, Mr Faraday. If you want any amplification after, I'll pick you up on the way back. I live in a lodge down by the main gates.'

'All right,' I said. 'If there's such strict security here why keep the gates open?'

Kempton nodded, his eyes bright as he studied me.

'We got lots of electronic gadgets, Mr Faraday. I could have picked you up half a mile away even if you hadn't come by automobile.'

'You still haven't answered my question,' I said.

He had a tight smile on his face now.

'You heard the story about the monkey and the gourd, Mr Faraday. It's an old one but worth repeating. There's something in the gourd the monkey wants but when he gets his paw in and clenches it into a fist he's trapped

6

because hc won't let go. It's not an exact analogy but it'll do in this case.'

I looked at Kempton for a long moment. He was becoming more interesting by the minute.

'What is it you're trying to tempt in here, Mr Kempton?'

He shook his head slowly, his eyes wary.

'Ask Miss Billington, Mr Faraday. Or better still, Mr Zangwill himself. It's more than my job's worth to talk out of turn.'

'Fair enough,' I said. 'See you on my way out.'

'I'll be here,' he said gravely.

I could feel his eyes boring into my back all the way over toward the big front door.

2

I rang the brass bellpush set in the old-fashioned circular brass mount and stood listening to its sonorous pealing inside the mansion, backgrounded by the lonely pumping of my heart and the melancholy patter of falling rain. It seemed to sum up the whole of my life. So far. You got one of those moods, Faraday, I told myself. One of those days, come to that.

Nothing was happening inside the house so I turned. The big man was still standing just within the vast porch, at the edge of the steps. He had been joined by the black Dobermann

7

now. The dog stood like it was carved out of solid coal, only its eyes alive, as it stared at me. The man and the dog looked like one of those china conversation pieces they sometimes have on the edge of ashtrays which are so extravagantly priced they're never used by the owners.

Kempton smiled encouragingly.

'Hit it again, Mr Faraday,' he called. 'It's a big house and Miss Billington has a long way to go.'

I nodded, hitting the bell again. This time I heard sharp, hurried footfalls on the parquet within. I gave a quick glance around but both the big man and the Dobermann had disappeared. The place was beginning to get on my nerves. And old man Zangwill's case hadn't even started yet.

The girl who opened the door to me was so unexpected in that place that I could only gape at her. She was of medium height, very slim but with curves in all the right places. Her hair was a deep shade of brown and fell in soft waves about her face. She wore some sort of severely tailored dress that was made of expensive material and caught in at the waist with a black leather belt.

She had the sort of finely chiselled face that you dream about or that you very occasionally see, about once every fifteen years, in the movies. It was the sort of beauty that's very hard to describe but which hits you when you encounter it in real life. Those were the only details I caught as she opened the massive, heavily carved door. That and the fact that she had eyes of so deep a shade of blue that they were more or less violet.

She had a low, breathless voice to go with the rest of her. Like everything else, it fitted perfectly.

'Mr Faraday? Mr Zangwill told me you were expected.'

'That's right,' I said. 'You'd be Miss Billington?'

She nodded almost shyly, like I was the host and she the visitor.

'Do come in. I'm so sorry you've had to walk up in such weather. Mr Zangwill insists on taking certain precautions and he has a sort of mania about invasion of privacy.'

She smiled briefly, exposing the flash of perfect teeth.

'So no cars. Except for mine and his own on the very brief visits he makes to the outside world.'

She led the way into a large, inner lobby which had heavy glass doors separating it from the hall of the house proper. She took my raincoat from me and hung it on a row of teak pegs projecting from the panelling of the right hand wall. There was nothing else hanging there, not even a stick in the stand that was screwed to the wall beneath.

There was highly polished teak parquet

9

beneath our feet and it was the girl's high-heeled shoes I'd heard clicking across it. Now that we were in the light I could see her face more clearly. I figured she was probably about twenty-five, though in certain attitudes she looked no more than eighteen. She flushed slightly beneath my appraisal and let go the sleeve of my raincoat.

'You'd probably like some tea and a chance to dry out before you see Mr Zangwill, Mr Faraday. We could go to my office.'

'That would be fine,' I said gallantly.

The girl opened the glass doors and I went on through. I waited for her in an enormous hall that had black and white tile flooring; heavy panelling of some light, exotic wood; large oils in gold frames hanging everywhere; cut flowers in china bowls on low tables and a graceful curving staircase going up to the right. The whole place looked like a left-over set from *Gone With the Wind*.

I heard the click as the key turned in the lock and I looked at the girl sharply. My surprise must have shown in my eyes for she said, almost apologetically, 'Mr Zangwill insists on it, Mr Faraday. I think you will understand a little more after our talk.'

'So it isn't just a social occasion ?' I said.

The Billington girl flushed again.

'Mr Zangwill has asked me to acquaint you with certain facts, Mr Faraday,' she said softly. 'He thinks you will appreciate his situation a

10

little better by the time you get to see him.'

'Sure,' I said. 'Your man in the grounds was equally mysterious.'

The Billington number led the way across the hall, her heels tapping rhythmically over the tiling. She had very nice legs now that I could see them properly.

'Kempton? He's a very good man. Specially selected by Mr Zangwill. You won't get much out of him.'

'So it seems,' I said. 'He spoke of drawing people in but so they would never get out.'

The girl smiled mysteriously.

'It's true enough, Mr Faraday,' she said simply. 'He told you his analogy of the monkey and the gourd, I suppose.'

'He did,' I said. 'It begins to sound like a guided tour.'

The girl gave a low laugh which echoed round the staircase.

'I must disabuse you of that notion, Mr Faraday. Just in here. Tea will be along in a few minutes. I rang as soon as I heard you at the front door.'

She opened a polished teak door that was set in the staircase wall and I followed her through into what was obviously the main study of the house. It was a huge, panelled room, got up in unostentatious good taste, with a gallery running round, and thousands of books in hand-crafted teak bookcases that ran round all four sides. The only break was with the big stone fireplace in front of us, though even here the gallery, with its bookshelves, continued above.

There was a fragrant fire of logs burning low in the iron grate basket and the girl led the way over toward it. In the centre of the room was set up a large Directoire-style desk that was piled with books and papers; there was a modern metal waste basket; two electric typewriters; file cabinets; an electric copying machine and a lot of stuff that normally I'd have expected to have seen only in downtown L.A.

The girl evidently noticed my surprise because she said with another hesitant smile, 'I did say this was my office, Mr Faraday. We do get through a lot of work in here.'

'I don't doubt it, Miss Billington,' I said.

I went over toward the fireplace and smoothed back my hair. Drops of moisture fell sputtering on to the logs.

'Forgive me,' the Billington number said. 'If you'd prefer to wash-up before tea?'

'Don't bother,' I said. 'I'll be all right in a minute or two.'

I stood in front of the fire, feeling the heat beginning to dry out my trousers and the collar of my jacket, slowly taking in the details of the room. The girl had placed a low table about six feet from the fireplace and now she dragged two chairs over. The far door had already opened and a tall, severe-looking woman with powdered grey hair was gliding in, wheeling an elaborate tea-trolley on noiseless castors.

'This is Mrs Meakins, our housekeeper,' the girl explained. 'She runs the whole place here, Mr Faraday.'

The woman bowed distantly, a faint smile hovering at the corners of her mouth.

'I'm sure Miss Billington exaggerates, Mr Faraday. I do my best.'

'I'm sure,' I said.

I stood and watched while the two women set the table out with a lot of silver things and trays loaded with small china plates of sandwiches and cakes. This was so far from my normal routine I figured I might have strayed into an early Ronald Colman movie. I'd be getting to the gritty stuff later so I enjoyed it while I had it.

Mrs Meakins finished fussing about at last and said to the girl, 'There's plenty more hot water if you require it, Miss Billington. You have only to ring.'

She glided off out as silently as she'd come.

The girl turned to me, giving a smile of great beauty.

'You wouldn't think this whole atmosphere was steeped in murder and violent death.'

CHAPTER TWO

1

We stared at one another for what seemed like half an hour. It could have been only a few seconds in reality because I saw a piece of blazing log start to fall from the fire-basket as she began to speak and it had only hit the hearth and rolled over before I made my reply.

'I thought this place was too good to be true.'

The girl sat down with a smooth, rippling movement in the armchair behind the small table and fussed around with cups and the silver tea-pot.

'It's always a mistake to go on first impressions,' she said. 'Sugar and milk?'

'Both, please,' I said.

I could hear the heavy ticking of a clock now and eventually I traced it to a shadowy corner of the room where a large, cased eighteenth century job with a glass panel showed me the brass pendulum slowly describing its dull arc.

'You mentioned murder and violence, Miss Billington,' I said.

The girl shook her head with a slight air of impatience.

'Let's leave it until we've had our tea. Wouldn't you rather call me Laura?'

I glanced again round the silent room with its panelling and thousands of books and the soft fire burning in the grate. The only thing missing was the oil painting over the fireplace. The girl smiled her unique smile as she handed me the cup.

'I know what you're thinking, Mr Faraday. But I don't look the least bit like Gene Tierney and you're no Dana Andrews.'

I sipped at the tea. It was faintly perfumed and very good.

'Thanks very much,' I said.

The corners of Laura Billington's mouth turned down with a little moue.

'Please don't think me rude, Mr Faraday. You're very personable. It's just that neither of us has the charisma of film stars. And that's a crack often made by people who come out here.'

I looked at her over the rim of my cup.

'So you do get people out here? Why don't you call me Mike if we're going informal?'

The girl nodded.

'From time to time, Mike. I'm talking about people who come here. Mr Zangwill hasn't quite scared everyone off.'

'I should hope not,' I said. 'Otherwise you'd find it pretty lonely.'

The girl's eyes held mine for a long second.

'It's lonely enough,' she said softly. 'Will you have some cucumber sandwiches? They're really good. Mrs Meakins serves only the best.'

'I'm sure,' I said in my best P.G. Wodehouse manner. Laura Billington smiled mischievously.

'You'd better take half a dozen. They are rather on the small side.'

There was silence between us, broken only by the faint crackling of the fire and the pattering of the rain at the windows. I could have gotten used to this sort of life pretty quickly and I wasn't looking forward to the grit in the machine Zangwill's problems were likely to produce. The girl must have been of the same mind because she maintained her silence and kept her eyes averted as the minutes ticked by.

We were on the small, home-made iced cakes before she spoke again.

'You're familiar with Mr Zangwill's history, Mr Faraday?'

I shook my head.

'I know very little about him, really. I believe he made a fortune in zinc in the twenties, didn't he? When the going was good. And I heard he married some society beauty and they had great parties here in the thirties.'

The girl nodded, looking at me with respect.

'You know a great deal more than most people. I'm surprised that anyone would remember. And for such a young man . . .'

I grinned.

'My secretary keeps excellent files, Laura. And I saw a TV documentary last year in

16

which his name was mentioned. Shots of this house were included.'

The girl sat up straight in the armchair, her cup poised halfway to her lips.

'I didn't know that.'

I put my own cup down with a faint chinking in the silence of the study.

'It was nothing to do with him, really. It was a film about F. Scott Fitzgerald and the Jazz Age. This house was included as an example of the big houses of the period and of the type of parties given.'

The girl's brow smoothed as though by an invisible sponge.

'I see. It was a pity, nevertheless. Mr Zangwill would have been deeply interested in such a programme.'

I looked at her sharply.

'There was something about his wife, wasn't there? Not in the TV film, of course. But in the newspapers of the thirties.'

The girl put her small pink hands nervously on her thighs and moved them up and down, making little stirring noises with the material. It set my nerves aflame and suddenly turned her into a desirable sexual object.

Maybe she became aware of this for the violet eyes held my gaze in turn and she stopped the movements abruptly.

'It wrecked Mr Zangwill's life. His wife was killed in a riding accident back in 1938.'

'I'm sorry,' I said.

17

The girl had her eyes up on the gallery above my head now.

'I know you are, Mike. But it was a long time ago.'

'Mr Zangwill never married again?' I said.

Laura Billington shook her head.

'He shut himself away from the world. Became an almost total recluse. There was only one woman for him and his life died with hers.'

I nodded, reaching for my package of cigarettes.

'I've heard of such things,' I said. 'A rare love. Such a marriage leaves one a vulnerable hostage to fortune.'

The Billington number raised her eyebrows.

'You're quite a philosopher.'

'I didn't mean to be,' I said.

The girl shrugged.

'You were right, anyway. It wasn't until I arrived here five years ago that the house started to come to life again.'

'What is your function?' I said.

There was a slightly defensive expression on Laura Billington's face now.

'Purely secretarial,' she said softly. 'Mr Zangwill's business affairs were in some disorder, following decades of neglect. He is still immensely rich, of course, but none of the potential of his interests had been realized.'

'You soon changed that,' I said.

The girl nodded solemnly.

18

'It was my function here. After that, Mr Zangwill seemed to regain his zest for living. He's already written his memoirs with my assistance, which a major New York publisher is bringing out next year. And now he's hard at work on a definitive history of the U.S. metal mining industry.'

'Bully for him,' I said.

The girl smiled faintly.

'That's as far as it goes, Mike. At least until six months ago.'

I leaned back in the armchair and lit a cigarette at the girl's extended permission. I feathered out blue smoke up toward the gallery and the serried ranks of books.

'That's when the trouble started?' I said.

The girl suddenly put her hands together and clasped them until the skin showed white.

'Exactly.'

I looked at her through the thin veils of smoke.

'We'd better get at it, then,' I said. 'That's what I'm here for.'

2

I moved in my chair and flicked my ash into the smouldering heart of the log fire. My clothing had dried off nicely now and I felt almost human again.

'Before I start,' the girl said, 'you're maybe

curious as to why Mr Zangwill asked me to see you first.'

'It had crossed my mind,' I said. 'I don't want to have to work through the same material twice.'

Laura Billington shook the mass of soft brown hair from her eyes. The gesture reminded me of something I'd seen an actress do in a movie a long time ago. I'd forgotten now but I'd get to it in time. If I was on the case long enough, that is.

'We won't do that, Mr Faraday. I said Mr Zangwill is a recluse and I meant exactly that.'

'It seemed pretty urgent from what my secretary said,' I told her. 'Mr Zangwill rang himself, she tells me.'

The Billington number nodded.

'That is very unusual, Mr Faraday. I was startled, I can assure you. Apparently he came across your name in a telephone directory. Then he rang one or two old friends to get a rundown on you.'

She stopped and leaned back in her chair, her body vibrant and taut, her deep violet eyes raking me over.

'It sounds flattering,' I said. 'I gather he got a favourable report on my operation.'

'The best,' the girl said.

She moved her glance over to a big leaded window at the far side of the great room where the garden sat patiently under the falling curtain of rain. The window was bow-fronted too and looked like something out of an old print. It would have cost millions to reproduce such a house out here at today's prices.

'You can see my difficulties,' the Billington girl went on. 'I'm supposed to open your mind to every possibility, but I don't know all the details myself. Then Mr Zangwill will see you, presumably to release some more specific information and authorize you to act for him.'

I leaned forward in my chair, my eyes studying the girl's face.

'It sounds a little involved,' I said. 'But not unknown in my experience. Is the old man in fear of his life? Or being shaken down for blackmail for something?'

Laura Billington smiled faintly.

'You're very blunt and direct, Mr Faraday.'

I grinned.

'I find it best in my business. I operate at the rough end of the market.'

She raised her eyebrows again.

'Meaning what?'

'Street level,' I said. 'Where blood flows and knuckles get split. It's no good us horsing around if I'm to help Mr Zangwill. If he's got something in his past that someone can put pressure on him for then I want to know about it. You mentioned murder a little earlier but you're pretty coy about going into the details.'

The girl's face went white and her fingers clenched and unclenched in her lap. She sat up straight in the chair and bit her lip. She looked pretty appealing like that.

'If I am, Mr Faraday, it's because I hardly know where to begin.'

I opened my mouth to speak again but she held up a small pink hand like she was Canute stilling the waves. Or not stilling them as the case may be.

'Hear me out, Mr Faraday. There is something like that. Mr Zangwill is in fear of his life. I have some notes on the matter. I'm sure we'll give you every co-operation.'

'That's more like it,' I said. 'And I think we agreed the name was Mike.'

The girl flushed.

'I'm sorry. Mike, then. Like I said this thing began some six months ago. Mr Zangwill started by being distant and furtive. I'd worked for years to get him to a normal frame of mind but he seemed to be regressing to the state he was in when I first came here.'

'Let's get down to basics,' I said. 'What was the staff position when you took up your post?'

The girl looked surprised but she wrinkled up her forehead as though she were thinking heavily. It didn't affect her good looks any.

'Much the same as at present, Mike, except for the chauffeur, who left a couple of years back. I do most of Mr Zangwill's driving now. Mrs Meakins was already here. There's Mrs Zaborski, a widow, who does the heavy work around the house. A gardener comes in every day. And Mr Kempton took charge of security.'

'Security?' I said. 'He already had the grounds staked out then?'

'That's right. There's a lot of valuable stuff here. Mr Kempton originally came from a security firm in L.A. Mr Zangwill found him so helpful he installed him in the lodge and he came to work here privately. We still get a relief in whenever he's sick or on holiday. And for his two days off a week, of course.'

'Of course,' I said. 'Mr Zangwill pays well?'

The girl turned down her eyes and critically examined the toecap of one of her immaculate polished leather shoes.

'Exceptionally well. I think you'll find that when you come to present your fee.'

'I haven't taken the case yet,' I said. 'Haven't got a case. And I have a set daily rate.'

The girl shrugged with a sinuous movement of her shoulders. It seemed to be one of her favourite actions. She leaned over to pour me another cup of tea from the silver pot. I was becoming quite an addict this afternoon. It must have been the rain. We were silent again until she'd finished pouring. I took another one of the small iced cakes she pressed on me.

'I think you'll take the assignment when you've heard me out. Mr Zangwill needs help badly.'

'All right,' I said. 'We've got the staff situation laid out. The same people now as five years ago. Except for the chauffeur. Mr Zangwill was always security conscious. And six months ago he began to change. Distant and furtive I think you said.'

The girl laughed softly.

'I think you'll do. You have a photographic memory.'

'You haven't told me anything yet. I want something concrete to go on. It started with letters, didn't it?'

There was slight shock in the girl's eyes.

'How did you know that?'

'Such situations usually do,' I said. 'Containing threats to his life?'

The girl swallowed, her eyes far away, seemingly focused on some distant object.

'He never showed me the letters but I know they greatly disturbed him.'

I had my notepad out now, started jotting down a few particulars.

'Did he say specifically that his life was in danger?'

The girl shook her head.

'Not at that stage. A couple of weeks ago he took me into his confidence.'

'You didn't know who the notes were from?'

She shook her head.

'He wouldn't say. I believe he burned most of them.'

'That's a pity,' I said.

There was another long silence.

'Go on,' I said at last. 'There must be more.'

The girl clasped her hands together like she'd come to a decision.

'There is, Mike. About three weeks ago someone tried to get into the grounds at dead of night. There was some shooting. Kempton must have frightened the intruder off because he left without taking anything.'

'How do you know he came to take something?' I said. 'It might have been the man who threatened Mr Zangwill.'

The girl nodded.

'You're right, of course. I was just talking. No-one was hurt, so far as we know. The person in the grounds got away in a car parked on the road outside.'

'What was Mr Zangwill's reaction?' I said.

'He was in a terrible way for a couple of days. He seemed to shrink into himself. And he ordered a lot more expensive electronic equipment.'

I leaned over and tipped off more of my ash into the fireplace.

'The man didn't get as far as the house?'

The girl shook her head.

'The dog was just too late to catch him. Normally he roams the grounds at night but it was extremely wet that evening and he was locked indoors. Mr Zangwill has a report from Kempton if you want to see it.'

'I shall want to see it,' I said. 'I'm still waiting to hear the rest.'

The girl cleared her throat nervously and

picked up her cup again.

'Like what?'

'Like murder and violence,' I said. 'This thing doesn't really hang together. And you're not telling it very well.'

The girl's violet eyes were angry now.

'I'm sorry,' she said in a stiff, chintzy voice.

'Why didn't Mr Zangwill call the police in?' I said.

'He was insistent that we shouldn't,' the girl said.

A little of the anger was still in her voice.

'That sounds as though he had something to hide,' I said.

The girl's eyes were glinting but whether with anger still or puzzlement I couldn't tell. It was dark in the room and there were no lamps lit so we made do with the light from the leaded windows and that from the fire. It suited me all right; it must have been the sort of scene that the Victorians were familiar with.

'All rich men have something to hide,' the Billington girl said. 'Mr Zangwill is probably no exception. Besides, what could we have told the police? They get thousands of intruder calls like that every year.'

I nodded, leaning forward to tip the ash off my cigarette again. She had a point there.

'Fair enough,' I said.

I kept my eyes fixed on the delicate oval of her face.

'Who do you think it was?'

26

Laura Billington shook her head.

'I don't know enough about the set-up, Mike.'

'Come on,' I said. 'You know more about Zangwill probably than anybody. Make an inspired guess.'

Her eyes were turned sideways now, toward the fire. She studied the small red and blue flames like the answer to things that were troubling her lay there.

'You didn't see Mr Zangwill,' she said at last. 'I've never seen such terror on a human face. All I know is he'd had threats to his life. Then someone tried to get in the grounds at two in the morning. Whoever it was actually fired shots at Kempton before escaping.'

I studied my toecaps. Like always they were scuffed.

'That's solid enough,' I said. 'Why don't you keep the gates shut and locked at night? Or does the monkey and gourd theory still hold after dark?'

The girl shook her head.

'The gates are locked, winter and summer, at dusk. They're left open only during the day, when Kempton or the other guards are around.'

'That makes sense,' I said. 'I'm still waiting for the rest.'

Laura Billington bit her lip. She had an attitude again like she was listening for something.

27

'Would you like some more tea?' she said irrelevantly.

I shook my head.

'I'm still waiting for some specific detail on this case. I've got two solid facts so far.'

The girl's face was worried.

'I'm telling it very badly,' she said.

'You're not, Laura,' I said. 'You're just not telling enough of it.'

She smiled then. I fixed my eyes up on the gallery.

'You still haven't explained precisely why you didn't call the police. If shots were fired . . .'

The girl caught her breath with a little implosive sound in the dusk of the library.

'Mr Zangwill was keen to,' she said quickly. 'He wanted to call in the police after I was attacked but I insisted myself that we handle things discreetly. I suggested a private detective, but it was only today that he acted.'

I sat bolt upright in my chair and stared at her. She flushed and moved uncomfortably in her own seat.

'So you were attacked?' I said.

Her eyes were very bright now.

'Last week.'

I stared up at the gallery and sighed.

'This thing is becoming a tangle,' I said. 'Don't you think you'd better come on down, Mr Zangwill, and let me have it from the horse's mouth?'

CHAPTER THREE

1

The girl's face was a mask of astonishment. There was a heavy silence broken by a clatter from the gallery. A shock of white hair lifted itself from the darkness of the lower bookshelves.

'I should have known better, Mr Faraday,' said a rueful voice. 'But I wanted to see what sort of man you were.'

'You'd have found out more with a couple of minutes' conversation face to face,' I said. 'And we've wasted all this time with that story of Miss Billington's.'

The girl had gotten up from her chair.

'Everything I've told you is the truth, Mr Faraday. It's just that I was inhibited by Mr Zangwill's presence. I'm sorry for the pretence, if it means anything to you.'

'It does,' I said.

There was more clattering from the gallery as old man Zangwill descended a narrow circular stair that led down to the floor of the library. He came forward behind the girl, holding out his hand in a courteous, old-world gesture. He was a remarkable sight. He was all of six feet four inches in height and age had done little to stoop him.

He had frank, open features with clear blue eyes that were almost as remarkable as the girl's. His snow-white hair gave him a dusty and faded look, but his brown face with the square jaw was alert enough. He wore a heavy tweed suit that hung loosely on his gaunt frame and he had on one of those brown, hand-knitted ties that I thought had gone out with D.H. Lawrence. Not that Lawrence's work has gone out; just the man himself.

When he got closer to me I could see that he was wearing plus fours too; they were of the same material as the coat, which had made me think he was wearing a suit. That evoked the twenties too and for a brief second, as we shook hands, his timorous smile reminded me of blurred old newspaper photographs of the late W. R. Hearst. But this character was far more affable and less ruthless.

He waved me back into my chair and courteously waited until the girl had re-seated herself before he himself slumped into a leather armchair that stood midway between the small table and the fire. He must have been around eighty yet all his movements were alert and eager, like those of a man in his thirties. He must have been really something when he was young.

The girl held up the tea-pot but he waved it away.

'Already had mine in the dining-room, Laura. I took it early today because I wanted to see Mr Faraday before he started bombarding me with questions.'

'Do you find it so hard to answer them?' I said.

The girl shot me a warning glance and I saw a swift look of understanding pass between her and the old man.

'You don't really understand, Mr Faraday. I live much out of the world, as Laura here has told you.'

He gave a heavy sigh.

'This interview today is an ordeal, really. I wish you fully understood. To expose myself and my thoughts is painful to one of my generation. And this whole situation is so deadly in one way and yet so ridiculous in others.'

I flipped my cigarette butt into the heart of the dying fire. The girl sat at the apex of the triangle made by the three of us and listened to the conversation with bright eyes.

'Anyone would think you were the employee and I the employer,' I told him. 'You're hiring me, after all. You act as though I posed some sort of threat to you.'

The old man gave a short, barking laugh.

'That's very good, Mr Faraday. You do, old chap, you do.'

He rubbed his big hands together in the gloom and the silence with a curiously harsh rasping noise. I guessed then that he worked with his hands and that he might still be

31

immensely strong, despite his advanced age.

'If you only knew the difficulties I have in communicating with people from the modern world.'

He shot an affectionate glance at the girl.

'Apart from Laura here. And my personal staff who have been with me for years.'

'Pretend I'm not here,' I said. 'Just talk to Miss Billington and I'll listen.'

He shook his head ruefully.

'But you are here, Mr Faraday. And I asked you here. And I should now have the courage and courtesy to take you into my full confidence. In the first place everything that Laura has told you has been the truth. I was threatened; an attempt was made to break in here; and this young lady was attacked a week ago tonight.'

'Yet you only call me in now,' I said.

Old man Zangwill gave another heavy sigh, his shoulders sagging as though with the weight of his problems.

'That is my fault, Mr Faraday, and I can only apologize. Laura insisted on my not calling the police on that occasion and I concurred.'

He turned appealing blue eyes to me.

'You see, Mr Faraday, we are peculiarly vulnerable here. The world has passed me by and I am content that it should be so. But if the police came here; if there were reports in the newspapers and the glare of publicity—

television even, then that would be absolutely intolerable.'

'In what way?' I said.

Another glance went between him and the girl.

'You disappoint me, sir. I thought I had made myself plain. I am still an enormously rich man. If attention is drawn to my wealth and my estate it may attract other people to try their luck.'

He made an eloquent gesture with his big, capable hands.

'All right,' I said. 'You want to be discreet. They don't get any discrecter than me.'

I glanced at my watch.

'I've been here over an hour and I've learned almost nothing so far. Like I said before, let's get down to it.'

2

The lamps were lit, my pencil went racing across the paper and Zangwill's voice droned on. He seemed to have lost his inhibitions now and the air was filled with the rich fragrance of his cigar-smoke. He'd back-tracked on the story and told it in his own words. Now we were getting on to fresh information and I wanted it all clear in my mind.

He broke off with an apologetic smile.

'I think Laura should tell the next part, in

her own words.'

'I was driving into town that night,' the girl said. 'I'd stopped at the lodge to give Kempton some instructions from Mr Zangwill.'

'So you were outside the security zone?' I said.

Zangwill leaned forward in his armchair until it creaked.

'You could call it that, Mr Faraday. You'll see when you go out. The lodge is in a small enclave, in its own grounds, and outside the main walls surrounding the house.'

'So there are no security precautions there?' I said.

The girl nodded.

'Exactly. But there are a lot of bushes and shrubbery round about which make the place gloomy and it was a dark night. I was getting back in the car when I saw a vague, shadowy figure in the passenger seat. I was halfway-in, halfway-out the driving side. I screamed and the thing turned.'

I stared at her for a long moment.

'Why do you say "thing" ?' I said.

The girl shuddered, her eyes seeking the old man in the armchair by the fireside, as though for reassurance.

'Because it had no face, Mr Faraday,' she said slowly. 'There was nothing but blackness and two white, staring eyes.'

I made a note on my pad.

'You realize, of course, that it was your

imagination,' I said. 'We're not dealing with ghosts. Whoever was in your car probably wore a mask made of some black material with two holes cut for the eyes. I'm not saying it wasn't a horrific experience but there's nothing out of the ordinary to anyone used to dealing with criminals.'

The girl made another funny little implosive noise as she sucked in her breath.

'Of course, you're right,' she said in a hurried voice.

'You must be because the thing struck at me. It caught my forehead and left a big bruise. I fell down by the side of the automobile and when I came around whatever it was had gone.'

'A horrible experience,' old Zangwill said in a rather quavery voice.

'I'm not denying that,' I said. 'Was there anything missing from the car?'

Laura Billington shook her head.

'Nothing that I could make out. I called Kempton and he searched around but he didn't find anything.'

'Where was the dog while all this was going on?' I said.

The old man broke in, his voice stronger now.

"We always keep the dog confined within the grounds, Mr Faraday. It would be a danger to the public otherwise.'

'That figures,' I said.

I made another note on the pad.

'We've had the violence and the threats,' I said. 'You mentioned murder earlier, Miss Billington.'

'Threats of murder, Mr Faraday,' the old man said gently. 'This used to be a happy house. Now it's a place of fear and suspicion.'

He rummaged around in the inner pocket of his capacious jacket.

'Here's one of the notes I got.'

He handed it me. It was on a rough sheet of blue stationery with the top edge torn, where it had been ripped hastily off the pad. The printed letters had been cut out of various newspapers; that was another old trick so I didn't waste time on it but studied the message.

'You didn't keep the envelope?' I said.

The old man shook his head.

'I'm afraid not. The thing came through the post in the ordinary way. It bore an L.A. postmark, like all the others. I destroyed the rest, I'm afraid.'

'How many were there?' I said.

'About half a dozen,' Zangwill said.

I studied the thing again; in uneven lines the letters, in various typefaces, spelled out: LEAVE HALF A MILLION IN USED NOTES INSIDE THE MAUSOLEUM. IF YOU DON'T YOU GET TO JOIN YOUR WIFE.

'Nice,' I said.

There was a heavy silence in the room, broken only by Zangwill getting up to put some more logs on the fire. He sat down again and stared at me grimly.

'The messages were all like this?' I said.

Zangwill nodded.

'On the same lines,' he said.

'I don't understand this bit about the mausoleum,' I said. 'And why would anyone expect you to put down that sort of money on a death threat? There doesn't seem any obvious advantage to me.'

I looked at him with what I hoped was an apologetic expression.

'Apart from keeping alive, that is.'

Before Zangwill could answer the girl interrupted.

'Mrs Zangwill is buried in the grounds,' she said softly. 'That was the mausoleum thcy were talking about.'

'They?' I said.

The girl flushed.

'The person or persons who compiled that note.'

'None of this makes sense,' I said. 'I could understand a threat and a demand for money. Even the death part. But why leave the cash in the mausoleum which is in the middle of a heavily guarded estate?'

'The whole thing is preposterous,' Zangwill said. 'I would never give in or pay such money under threat.'

He gave a deep sigh, his anguished eyes fixed on my face. 'You'll take the case, Mr Faraday.'

I stared at him, the cogs of my mind going round, finding nothing to grip on.

'I'll need to know a lot more about things first, Mr Zangwill,' I said. 'Sure, I'll take the case.'

CHAPTER FOUR

1

When I got outside again it was nearly dusk and the rain had stopped. The girl came down to walk with me to the gate. We'd chewed things over for half-an-hour or so longer but I couldn't get anything else out of either of them. Then the old man had made his excuses and left us, leaving the girl to write me out a cheque. It was a generous one too and it seemed to burn a hole in my wallet as it sat there.

'I'd like to have a look at this mausoleum before I leave,' I said.

Laura Billington shot me a startled glance.

'I don't know about that, Mike. I'd need Mr Zangwill's permission.'

'What the hell for?' I said. 'It's in the grounds, isn't it? How am I supposed to help either of you if I haven't got free access up here. I haven't a place to start at the moment. There's only this note and that won't tell me anything I don't know already.'

The old man had given me that as well and I had it in my pocket. The girl had put on a short blue jacket with silver buttons, like a schoolgirl's blazer and now she dug her hands deep in her pockets like she'd come to a momentous decision. She put her head on one side as she surveyed me.

'You're right, of course. It's only about two hundred yards. We'll have to go right round the house.'

'Fine,' I said.

There was a heavy silence between us as we worked round.

'I'll have to come out again tomorrow,' I said. 'I haven't finished with Mr Zangwill yet. There isn't nearly enough to go on.'

The girl's violet eyes looked almost black as she stared at me.

'You think he hasn't told you everything?'

'You're joking,' I said. 'He hasn't told me anything. What am I supposed to do with this situation? The note tells me nothing. It could have been written by anyone, posted from anywhere in the L.A. basin. I've nowhere to begin.'

The girl gave a faint sigh. We were walking along a narrow zig-zag path now, made of heavy paving stones, that was raised up over well-clipped lawns. The steely sheen of a lake glinted in the distance.

'I suppose you're right, Mike.'

'You bet I am,' I said. 'Unless Mr Zangwill can come up with something all I can do is to wait for another attack on someone out here. And I don't do bodyguard work.'

The girl's face had turned white. She stopped in the shelter of a little wooden ornamental pavilion. She bit her lip and took my arm.

'Come in here out of the wind for a moment. We can talk better.'

I faced her in the dimness of the interior which smelt of stale cigarette smoke, damp earth and mould.

'There is something else but I can't tell you. Mr Zangwill does know more than he's told you. He's a curious, reticent man.'

I lit a cigarette and feathered out blue smoke at the gathering dusk outside the pavilion.

'What is that supposed to mean?'

The girl shifted uneasily from one foot to the other.

'I can't elaborate now. It must come from Mr Zangwill himself. I can only point you in the right direction.'

'I'm waiting,' I said.

There was another awkward silence as we stood there, the gusting of wind at the roof of the wooden structure seeming like an intrusion.

'Ask him if he has any estranged relatives,' the girl said. 'That's the best I can do.'

I stared at her for a long moment, the cogs of my mind moving sluggishly.

'All right,' I said. 'I was conned into taking this crazy case by both you and the old man. I'm due out here again at three tomorrow. If I don't get anything definite to work on by then I'm going to tear up the cheque.'

Laura Billington looked startled, her violet eyes wide and strange.

'You can't do that, Mike,' she said in a shocked voice. 'Not give up the case.'

I shook my head.

'I can and I will,' I said. 'I've nothing to go on. There isn't a case from my point of view.'

The girl came up close and put her hand on my arm again.

'There will be a case. I'll talk to Mr Zangwill tonight. He must be more frank with you.'

'That's more like it,' I said. 'Now let's have a look at this mausoleum before we both get rheumatism.'

2

The girl smiled faintly, stepping out the shelter. It had started to rain again.

'It's just a few yards more. Over there at the edge of the lake.'

We went on a short distance and there was a break in the trees. At the edge of the steel-grey sheet of water a big white building was slowly composing itself out the melancholy shroud of falling water. It was coming on nicely now.

We went on round, walking faster, the rain starting to penetrate. Already I regretted coming out here, a dozen unanswered questions hammering around inside my skull. The whole thing seemed screwy; apart from the fact that Zangwill felt his life threatened; that he'd had notes; that someone had shot at Kempton; and that the girl had been attacked; there was nothing I could get hold of in the case at all.

The facts as presented by the old man and the girl added up to a lot from their point of view; but I had no leads, nowhere to go and nothing that pointed to anybody. I was only coming out to look at the mausoleum through sheer politeness. I didn't expect to learn anything.

Something of my thoughts must have shown on my face because the girl looked at me anxiously. It was true I was keen to get away; something might come to me back in the office. And it was certain Stella would have some ideas about the set-up. She always did have; and nine times out of ten she'd pointed me in the right direction.

Our feet gritted dismally on the gravel as we rounded the end of the lake. The wind was directly in our faces now, which added to the pleasure. A shadow flitted across the middle distance; the great black Dobermann froze in the middle of the lawn, his skin glistening like black silk in the rain.

He looked at us sullenly, his eyes glowing like coals; the girl had stopped too and she took my arm. The dog was standing stock-still, one paw poised in mid-flight like something carved in rock.

'Kempton's about somewhere,' the girl whispered. 'It's not safe to move under these circumstances when the dog's on its own.'

I looked at her disbelievingly.

'You don't mean to say there's danger to you as well?'

The girl nodded.

'These dogs are trained to answer to only one man. That man is Kempton. We're quite safe as long as we keep perfectly still.'

'Seems to me there's more danger inside the estate than out,' I said.

The girl smiled faintly.

'You may be right.'

The dog suddenly pirouetted like he was on a wire. He went off like a rocket, passing round the end of the lake.

'Kempton's seen us,' the girl said. 'He's signalled him back.'

We were up close to the mausoleum now. It was a not unattractive building but its blanched marble made it look like an off-white wedding cake. There was a sort of cupola over the entrance and a bronze grille round. The girl led the way with quick, confident steps. We were on the marble paving under the overhang of the monument now and sheltered from the rain.

There were big bronze railings at the front and I had the strange feeling that Zangwill had designed the place like this so that the occupant of the tomb could get a good view of the lake and the small island that showed up as a black circlet in the middle. The girl opened the massive bronze catch of the gate and it went back on well-oiled hinges. We were in the dry, airy interior; light came in through circular glazed interstices in the marble high up.

The sarcophagus itself, made of polished red granite and only slightly less impressive than Napoleon's tomb in the Invalides, was simply fashioned in the shape of a casket with large sets of rings each side. It rested on a white marble plinth on which was engraved in plain gold lettering: *Erected by her sorrowing husband, Adrian Zangwill, this monument to his beloved wife, Gloria Zangwill, died April 11th, 1939, in her forty-second year.* A single line underneath proclaimed: *Requiescat In Pace.*

'What do you think of it?' Laura Billington whispered.

'It's all right if you like that sort of thing,' I

said. 'It doesn't do much for me.'

I stared at the memorial again.

'He seems to think more of himself than his wife.'

The girl had a shocked expression in her eyes. She was getting pretty good at these changes of mood.

'I don't think I quite understand, Mike.'

'Look at the inscription,' I said. 'It will come to you.'

I walked around and left her standing there. The sarcophagus was broadside on to the lake at the open end of the dome and on the reverse side, facing the curved opposite wall I found a bronze grille covering a niche in the white marble plinth. Above it was a circlet containing a bronze relief likeness of Zangwill's wife. It had been carried out by a first-rate artist and I stood looking in silence at the striking woman depicted.

The girl had joined me now.

'Quite a looker, wasn't she?'

I nodded.

'You can say that again.'

I turned my attention to the bronze grille, putting my hand on it. It swayed slightly and as I exerted pressure it came away on hinges, revealing the niche within.

'What's this for?'

'Mr Zangwill and the household staff put floral tributes here on the anniversary of her death.'

I closed it again, stood looking at it thoughtfully.

'That's where the note said the money was to be left?'

The girl nodded.

'According to Mr Zangwill. You must admit it's a pretty good place.'

'But vulnerable,' I said. 'Especially as the entrance door's not locked. So far as I'm concerned it just adds to the general unsatisfactoriness of the whole case.'

'I'm sure you'll puzzle it out, Mike,' the Billington girl said.

I looked at her sharply in the dimness of the memorial chamber but I couldn't detect any irony in her tones.

3

We went out then. There was no point in hanging around. Halfway back to the main gate we met Kempton, striding along in his dripping slicker. He tipped the edge of his wide-awake hat to the girl with his fingers and looked warily at me. He wasn't carrying the shotgun but I could see the unmistakable bulge of a pistol under his oilskin. There was no sign of the dog but I guessed he wouldn't be far away.

'I understand you had some trouble with an intruder,' I said.

His eyes sought the girl's face but she said quietly, 'You can speak freely to Mr Faraday. Mr Zangwill's retained his services to inquire into the circumstances.'

'He already phoned the lodge,' Kempton said harshly. 'That's why I'm here.'

I waited for his reply and he went on, after looking at the girl.

'Nothing much to tell. I was awakened by one of the alarms around two a.m. My indicator board showed someone had got over the wall at the other end of the estate. I put on a slicker and got down there fast.'

'I understand it was a rainy night,' I said.

Kempton nodded.

'Like now. Satan was tied up in the kennel. I thought it would save time if I went on down to the place the alarm indicated, rather than stay to let the dog loose.'

'Mr Zangwill told me there were some shots fired.'

Kempton fixed his eyes stonily on the sopping foliage in the middle distance.

'I found a guy in the bushes halfway between the wall and the house. He fired a pistol at me. I fired back. I wasn't carrying the shotgun because I had a long way to run and there was the consideration of the weight.'

'You didn't see who it was?'

The big guard shook his head.

'It was too dark. It was just a black shadow really. He fired again and I got another one off before he melted back into the bushes.'

'So you just exchanged two shots?' I said.

The strong yellow teeth glinted in Kempton's mouth as he drew his lips back in a mirthless smile.

'That's right, Mr Faraday. So far as I could make out I didn't hit him. And his shots certainly went a mile wide of me.'

The girl moved closer to me like Kempton's words were having an effect on her. She gazed round the sodden bleakness of the estate as if she could see the whole thing in front of her.

'I knew roughly the spot in the wall the guy was making for,' Kempton went on. 'Our alarm system indicates things like that.'

He shrugged, his eyes still focused far away.

'I heard a car gun up long before I got there.'

'How high is the wall there?' I said.

'About twelve feet. Uniform all the way round,' he said. 'Except for the front.'

The big man grinned briefly.

'Like I said, we leave things easy there, to invite people in.'

I nodded.

'Just as you say. And how would this character have got over the wall?'

There was no hesitation in the big man's manner.

'He must have been a pro. It wouldn't have been difficult. My guess is a rope ladder with grapnel hooks. He would merely have to transfer it either side when he was astride the wall.'

He scuffed moodily at the sodden turf with one big boot.

'I found scratch marks in the moss on the top when I checked next day.'

'What's your theory?" I said.

Kempton looked from me to the girl.

'I don't have theories, Mr Faraday. I'm not paid to have them. I just guard the place.'

'But you must have some ideas of your own,' I said. 'What about the man who attacked Miss Billington here?'

Kempton shrugged again.

'Probably the same guy. But I wouldn't know why any more than you would.'

'Thanks a lot,' I said.

'Glad to have been of help,' he said. 'Now, if you don't want me any more, miss, I've got a patrol to carry out.'

The girl shook her head.

'That's all right, Kempton. I told Mr Faraday everything we know already.'

She paused and looked at me.

'Which isn't very much.'

The tall man touched his wide-awake with his right hand again and went striding out across the grass.

'I'll say good afternoon, then,' the girl said.

'You sure I won't be eaten on my way back to the main gate?' I said.

The girl smiled.

'I don't think so, but you have a point. I'll come down with you.'

She fell into step with me and we walked in silence for the next two hundred yards.

'Who guards the front while Kempton is checking the perimeter?' I said.

'Satan,' the girl said simply. 'He doesn't bother people on the way out unless Kempton specially alerts him. He's ready for unauthorized people coming in.'

'It all sounds very complicated to me,' I said.

We were crunching our way down the main drive now. It seemed like two days since I'd first arrived here. I looked at my watch surreptitiously. It was just over three hours as a matter of fact. The girl saw me through the wicket gate and extended a small, warm hand for me to shake.

'I'm sorry you're disappointed with the information you've been given.'

'That information's fine,' I said. 'It's the information I haven't got that's baffling.'

'I don't think I quite understand,' she said for the second time.

'Think about it,' I said. 'See you tomorrow.'

I went away down the sidewalk to where I'd parked the Buick, leaving her standing there in the damp greenness and the falling rain, a puzzled expression on her face. I had a lot to chew on myself as I drove on back in to L.A.

CHAPTER FIVE

1

'Well, well,' Stella said. 'The Tomb by the Lake. The only thing missing is La Belle Dame Sans Merci.'

'My,' I said, raising one eyebrow. 'We don't need her with you on the case.'

'Thanks a lot,' Stella said. 'So you won't be wanting coffee?'

'I take it all back,' I told her.

I sat at my old broadtop and frowned at the cracks in the ceiling, listening to her click-clacking across to the glassed-in alcove where we do the brewing-up. She put her head round the screen, the gold bell of her hair shimmering under the overhead lamp.

'I suppose this Billington girl was clothed in white samite?'

I grinned.

'If you thought I wouldn't get the reference you're missing out,' I told her. 'As a matter of fact she was clothed in a blue blazer the last time I saw her.'

Stella raised an elegant eyebrow in turn.

'That means she was a looker,' she told the filing cabinet. 'Normally you wouldn't have noticed.'

Sometimes Stella's too perceptive for my

51

book. I kept discreetly quiet. She came back and sat on the edge of my desk, swinging an elegant leg.

Today she wore pale blue slacks and a rust-coloured red silk shirt which pulled at her taut breasts. She had a gold locket on a chain round her neck which glittered as she moved. *That glittering taketh me also*, as the poet said so long ago. A brown leather belt with a gold buckle sat across her flat stomach. She smiled faintly, like she knew what I was thinking.

I turned my eyes off her and looked across to the window blind where a misty rain tapped sombrely at the glass. Stella interpreted my look correctly.

'Nice weather for the case,' she said.

I nodded.

'We only need Boris Karloff for the chief suspect and we got the set.'

Stella didn't say anything, just rose from the corner of the desk and went back to the alcove. I sat salivating, smelling the fragrant aroma of roast coffee beans and thought of all the hundreds of other times I'd sat here like this, on similar cases; not having any idea of the set-up; and how most of them had come out all right in the end. The cogs of my mind were turning over but they had nothing to grip on.

Stella was back with the coffee; she put the cup on my blotter, pushed over the biscuit tin. She went to fetch her own and then came and sat opposite me, in the client's chair. She stirred her cup, her eyes searching my face. I shook my head.

'It's no good asking me, honey. I've nothing to go on.'

Stella smiled.

'Don't anticipate my questions. I just wanted to get the facts straight.'

I took the first, tentative sip at my cup. Like always, the taste was great.

'There are no facts,' I said.

Stella shook her head, frowning.

'There are always facts, Mike, and you know it. All we've got to do is to put them together.'

I sat up straight in my chair and traded glances with her. Even that didn't put her off.

'I've looked up Adrian Zangwill's record, Mike. As soon as you phoned last night I got on to an old friend of mine.'

I stared at her without speaking.

'A financial journalist,' Stella went on patiently. 'He alerted me to a few points. I called in at the Central Library on my way in this morning, got them to make a few photostats of salient clippings from the late thirties.'

There was a faint clicking noise in the silence. I thought it was my lower jaw hitting the blotter but then I realized it was only my cup touching the saucer. Stella grinned at my expression.

'So what you've got from Zangwill's end

53

combined with what I've learned today should make a valuable basis for checking.'

She paused.

'To see if there are any discrepancies.'

I nodded.

'I see what you mean. Zangwill was enigmatic, to put it mildly.'

'You think he hasn't come clean with you?' Stella said.

I shrugged.

'I don't think he's told me all the facts, if that's what you're getting at. He's a cagey old bird. Most financiers are. On top of that his secretary tells me he's been an almost pathological recluse for decades.'

Stella tapped with pink-fingered nails on the surface of the desk.

'That mausoleum is a strange idea, Mike. And why would the writer of these letters want the money left there, on a closely-guarded estate?'

'Just the same point I made myself,' I said.

'Points to an inside job, Mike,' Stella said.

'Maybe,' I said.

Stella turned very blue eyes on me.

'The Billington girl knows a good deal about Zangwill's financial affairs. It wouldn't be the first time an employee has tried to rip off a millionaire employer. It would be the easiest thing in the world for her to get to that mausoleum under cover of darkness.'

'I hadn't overlooked that either,' I said. 'But

you're forgetting the guard dog and Kempton.'

Stella shook her head slowly.

'The dog was chained up indoors on wet nights, Mike,' she said. 'That would give some leeway, wouldn't it? On cold, wet nights like now, for instance. Let's just go through the case, point by point.'

I glanced at my watch. I had all the time in the world.

'Why not,' I said. 'I have nothing else to do.'

Stella shook her head again.

'There's a great deal to do, Mike,' she said calmly. 'It's all in the clippings. There was a time, in the late thirties, when Adrian Zangwill was in danger of going broke.'

2

I stared at her in silence, the cogs of my mind racing round now, without meshing at all.

'That sounds fantastic,' I said. 'Zangwill was the great mining millionaire of the thirties.'

There was a knowing glint in Stella's eyes.

'That doesn't mean he wasn't near to taking a nose-dive in the late thirties. He was heavily over-extended, even for a man of his diversified interests. They call it lack of cash-flow now. And that's not all.'

'There's more?' I said.

Stella looked at me, her eyes dancing.

'So you don't want to know?'

'I didn't say that,' I told her.

'Zangwill's wife was a millionairess in her own right. It was only her money saved his empire.'

The tapping of the rain at the windows seemed very loud now. I swivelled in my chair, focusing my gaze up to the cracks in the ceiling.

'You found out more in an hour than I got out of all that talk yesterday,' I said.

Stella grinned.

'We make a great team,' she said.

She got up, reached over for my empty cup, and went to the alcove. She brought it back and pushed over with it a small brown envelope which she'd already filed under Zangwill's name. I opened it and shook out the photocopies of a number of newspaper cuttings.

They were mostly from the business pages of financial journals, dating from 1938 and 1939. There were a couple of exceptions; these related to the sudden death in the riding accident of Zangwill's wife.

There were pictures of the couple; even at three removes from the original photograph I could see she was a striking woman all right.

'A looker,' I said.

Stella nodded. She went to sit back in the client's chair and cupped her chin in the palms of her hands.

'Those copies don't give half the story,

Mike.'

I frowned at the cuttings as I spread them out on the blotter.

'That accounts for Zangwill's grief, his reclusiveness and the mausoleum on the lake,' I said. 'It doesn't account for his terror at the first of those notes. There was nothing particular in the one I saw. Leastways, to justify the reaction described by the girl.'

There was a triumphant look in Stella's eyes now.

'You've noticed that, have you?'

'I'd have to be pretty dumb not to,' I said.

Stella smiled angelically.

'We'll let that pass,' she said.

I didn't bother to top it. I got out a cigarette from my pack and lit up. I feathered blue smoke at the ceiling, put the spent match-stalk in the earthenware tray on my desk and stared at the cuttings.

'We got a lot of disconnected pieces,' I said.

'We always have,' Stella pointed out. 'But at least you'll be better informed when you meet Zangwill again this afternoon.'

'I hadn't forgotten,' I said.

I went through the cuttings again. The first was by a financial journalist named Dalton which emphasized the financial crisis through which Zangwill's group of companies was going. I checked on the dates; Zangwill would have been about thirty-eight then. Stella sat silent as I went through all the photostat copies she'd put in the envelope.

I only understood about half of what I read; financial dealings are mostly Greek to me. I can barely count my small-change and the zinc and heavy metals companies which Zangwill headed at that time were involved in so many fiscal complexities it would have needed people like Keynes and Dr Friedmann to sort them out. But I got the message all right. During part of 1938 and the first half of 1939 Zangwill was balanced on a financial knife-edge.

After his wife's death he was in the clear. I put down the first batch of cuttings and stared at Stella.

'I take it Zangwill did benefit from his wife's estate?'

Stella nodded.

'To the tune of some two hundred million dollars, except for minor bequests to her sister and old friends. She was the elder daughter of an oil millionaire.'

'Laura Billington said it was a love-match,' I said.

Stella gave me an old-fashioned look. She's good at that.

'Cynicism doesn't become you, Mike. Nothing wrong in a millionaire marrying a millionairess, surely?'

'Maybe not,' I said. 'I wouldn't really know.'

I turned back to the cuttings again. These were of more interest to me. They were connected with Mrs Zangwill's sudden death, which made the front pages all right; the resulting inquest; and the terms of the will. Most of the stuff was more or less what Laura Billington had told me.

Zangwill's wife had gone out riding on the estate that afternoon. In those days the place was open house and despite Zangwill's affluence there were no guards or security precautions, apart from the usual burglar alarms and a link-up with a police office that the rich and the powerful usually have. From the cuttings I built up a picture which was fairly familiar to me from TV documentaries which covered the period.

Like a lot of people up there Gloria Zangwill rode both on public roads and bridle-paths as well as on the estate; that afternoon she kept within the grounds because it was a thundery, sultry day. Zangwill didn't like riding and had gone out for a walk some time earlier. Mrs Zangwill's horse had come back in an hour or so with the girth broken.

Zangwill arrived at the house about that time and as the servants were alarmed, a search was mounted, headed by her husband himself. In an hour or so her body was found at the edge of thick woodland. It seemed that she'd ridden into a heavy branch and been thrown off, snapping the girth at the same time. She'd died of a fractured skull, presumably from landing on one of the rocks which were scattered about the terrain there.

A verdict of accidental death had been returned and Zangwill, apart from his renewed business activity, had gone into virtual social seclusion. It appeared from what the financial reporter said that his fortunes would have been repaired anyway, as shortly after, with the beginning of war in Europe the prospects for metals revived and Zangwill's companies made another fortune through supplying materials for aircraft production and munitions.

I sighed and put the stuff away. Stella sat looking at me in silence with that wonderful tact of hers.

'You did well, honey,' I said. 'Nothing really startling but it fills in a lot of useful detail.'

'I thought so,' Stella said. 'Now all we have to do is to find out why someone is trying to rip him off; who the person is; why the money should have been left in the mausoleum.'

She stopped and looked at me dreamily, her chin still cupped in her hands.

'Why Zangwill's life is worth half a million bucks.'

She puckered her brow.

'Oh, I forgot,' she said brightly. 'And what the earlier notes contained that frightened Zangwill so badly.'

'Nothing to it,' I said modestly.

We were still sitting like that when the phone buzzed. Stella went over to her own desk while I sat on smoking and staring at the ceiling. That didn't seem to help any. Stella had the receiver covered with one hand. There was a curious expression on her face.

'Man on the phone, Mike. He won't give his name. Says he knows something about the Zangwill set-up. He's willing to do a little horse-trading.'

'The hell he is,' I said.

I picked up my own phone. The voice in the receiver was harsh and tinny like its owner was trying to disguise it. Stella had her own phone and was ready to take notes at her desk. Her eyes met mine interrogatively.

'Mr Faraday?'

'Speaking,' I said.

'It's about the Zangwill case. I know something that might make it worth your while to see me.'

'I didn't know there was a Zangwill case,' I said.

'Come on,' the voice said, a definite rasp in it now. 'We both know different. You were up there just yesterday. I could give you a useful short cut. That's worth quite a lot, isn't it?'

'Depends on the information,' I said. 'What's your suggestion?'

The voice sounded aggrieved.

'You don't sound enthusiastic, Faraday.'

'It's the weather,' I said. 'And don't suggest a lonely turnpike in all this rain. It's been done before. I usually dig myself out of a trash-can in some alley five hours later.'

There was a hoarse chuckle on the line now.

'You got a nice sense of humour, Mr Faraday. We'll get along fine.'

'Don't bank on it,' I said.

There was another heavy silence. I could see Stella's gold pencil describing arabesques on her pad.

'Get your young lady to take down this address. It's a rented bungalow. There'll only be me there. There's no danger. And I got a fresh bottle of bourbon we can split.'

'I won't argue with that,' I said.

I glanced at Stella. She was smiling to herself now.

'What's the address?' I said.

He gave it and Stella took it down. It was on a location I didn't know but I'd find it all right on the large-scale.

'It will take you about an hour to get there,' he said.

'Which means you're speaking from a call-box in town,' I said.

He chuckled again.

'Right, Mr Faraday. I have to be careful in my business. But it'll be worth your while. Meet me at three o'clock this afternoon.'

'I'm due out at Zangwill's again,' I said.

There was urgency in the voice now.

'Cancel it, Mr Faraday. You'll find our interview much more informative and worthwhile.'

'All right,' I said. 'I'll be there as near three as I can make it.'

'You won't regret it,' the voice said.

The line went dead. I put back the phone thoughtfully. Stella's eyes were shining.

'We progress already, Mike,' she said softly.

'Maybe,' I said. 'You'd better give Zangwill a ring. Tell him something came up on the case but don't tell him what. I'll get back to him tomorrow afternoon.'

'Will do,' Stella said. 'What will you be doing between now and three o'clock?'

I looked at the sheeting rain which made the boulevard outside look like the poor man's Venice.

'I'll think of something,' I said.

CHAPTER SIX

1

It was worse, if anything, on the road. I'd had a quick lunch at Jinty's and an ill-advised glass of lager after came back as a sour taste in my throat as I tooled the Buick off the main stem and on to a secondary road leading up into the hills. It had come on to rain harder than ever after lunch and I was drenched before I even made the Buick.

I was drying out nicely now though and had

the heater going in order to take some of the moisture out the atmosphere. The Buick was planing on sheets of water as I drummed up the hair-pins and the road ahead looked like some tropical sea-scape; the greenness of the surroundings drowned as though beneath the sea. You're getting in your Emily Dickinson mood again, Mike, I told myself.

As I negotiated the bends, keeping a sharp eye out for the clouds of spray from fruit trucks coming in the opposite direction, I reviewed the facts on Zangwill's case. That didn't take me long and I found my thoughts drifting. Particularly to Laura Billington. Not only because she was a desirable dish; I wondered what her part was in all this. Stella's words came back to me; could be she was involved in some way. It was obvious the old man was now wealthier than he'd ever been.

People come crawling out the woodwork when money of that order was concerned. I slowed a little, lit a cigarette and steered with one hand while I put my match-stalk in the dashboard tray. The rain came off the windshield like a waterfall. It was so heavy on the surface of the secondary road that I had to slacken speed even further to avoid drowning the engine. It can certainly rain in Southern California and today was a classic example.

I'd long given up looking in the rear mirror at the traffic behind; I couldn't have seen anything in the sheeting clouds of spray my tyres were throwing up and the sparse traffic was keeping well back out of my way in any case. This wasn't the afternoon for overtaking and no-one was trying. Which was surprising when one came to think of it.

I feathered out blue smoke, fumigating a couple of mosquitoes which were dancing a gavotte on the steering column, and looked for the sign-post giving the turn off. I had to slow almost to a crawl but, miraculously, I picked it out before I missed the small lane I wanted. I signalled, changed down and lumbered across in the blinding spray.

Once on the bumpy, undulating surface of the minor road I stayed in low gear and shuddered along at twenty miles an hour, between high earth banks clothed with semi-tropical vegetation. I was still going uphill and the trees crowded over so densely they blotted out the sky. I wound down the driving window an inch to get some air but had to shut it pretty quickly because so much water was coming in.

Then the trees thinned out, a smooth tarmac surface appeared and I was in what seemed to be a small suburban conurbation set down in nowhere. Delaware Heights appeared to be a thirties speculative builder's idea of a housing estate. It had that faded, passé air about it. But I guessed, nevertheless, that it was some smart fifties operator's idea to do a pastiche of the thirties and I was proved right by the materials in the houses.

Not that I had much time for the passing scenery. Most of it was drowned anyway. The bungalows were fairly substantial, but looking rundown and ill-tended. A couple had For Sale boards up in the front lots and the lawns of most looked like ill-tended paddocks.

I guessed most of them belonged to L.A. commuters who were away all day and were too tired when they got back in the evenings to keep their properties in order. It was a thought for the afternoon anyway. I had nothing much else to occupy my time with.

I tooled on down, looking for Oceana. I spotted it at the end, right in the far corner of a cul-de-sac; it was on its own, set back from a circular turn-round in the road, which had a strip of grass in the middle with a solitary street-lamp in the centre of it. I wondered how much it had cost the developers to have the mains run out here. Maybe that's why they'd failed. I had no doubt they would have failed.

Oceana had failure written all over it. It was appropriately named too. It was an off-white building with a green-tiled roof, that was set in too close to the overhanging trees and foliage. The location made it damp and claustrophobic. When I got out the car I found out why. It was the last practicable plot on the location for a house and when they'd laid out the garden in front—or leastways, planned it— they had to get the house in underneath a spiny ridge which came down off the foothills and which would have cost a fortune to excavate.

I wondered what my unknown friend was doing out here. I'd soon find out. I pulled the Buick up facing the end of the cul-de-sac and killed the motor. The silence crowded in, broken only by the heavy pattering of the rain on the roof of the car. I sat and finished my cigarette; it was ten of three and I'd made good time out here under the conditions today. The house sat there, shuttered and silent, not a sign of life. There wasn't a sign of life on the whole estate come to that, except for the scuttering of birds in the soaking undergrowth and the splashing of water down the storm-drains.

It would be death in life to live out here, Mike, I told myself. I could say that again. I refrained from doing so because the locale was too depressing as it was. I leaned forward and stubbed out my cigarette butt in the dashboard tray. The heavy bulk of the Smith-Wesson .38 in its nylon harness made a reassuring pressure against my chest muscles. I didn't know if it was going to be that sort of case but I'd decided to break it out from the small armoury I keep in a locked cupboard in my rented house over on Park West. I'd cut short my lunch and called there on my way out this afternoon.

It would be the best friend I'd got if anything broke. My informant hadn't sounded like a toughie but I didn't know who his principals might be. He may have been working on his own but one never knew. And I didn't understand what information he might have about Zangwill's set-up that would be worth anything. Not that I'd be paying. Zangwill would foot the bill if the information was worth it.

I wouldn't find out by hanging around here so I got out the Buick, slammed the door and sprinted up the concrete zig-zag path in front of the bungalow. It sat there damply and seedily and waited for me to come.

2

I was half-drowned before I hit the porch. I buttoned the bell and stood listening to the hissing of the rain and the thumping of my heart. Nothing broke the heavy silence except the rain and the faint sound of a car engine, far off. I hit the button again when the door was opened cautiously. It had been painted green once but the paint had blistered and it had a leprous aspect. A cadaverous face with deep-set eyes surveyed me from behind a heavy chain which secured the door.

'Expecting trouble?' I said.

The thin man shook his head slowly.

'I'm not looking for it. You're Mr Faraday?'

'I've had a hell of a wasted journey if I'm

not,' I said.

The bluish lips pulled back over the yellowing teeth. I was getting less enamoured of the interview with every second that passed.

'I'd like a look at some identification,' the thin man said. 'I'm in a delicate business.'

'I can imagine,' I said.

I fumbled in my inner pocket and got out my licence photostat. That's all I seemed to be doing the last couple of days. The thin man took it with a set of dirty fingernails and studied it in the crack of the door, his head on one side like it was printed in gold blocking on vellum. The licence, of course, not his head. He grunted and gave it back to me.

'I guess it'll have to do,' he said, like he was disappointed with my qualifications.

'I guess it will, unless you want to see my driver's licence,' I said. 'Do I get to come in or is this some sort of examination for the Coastguard Service?'

The thin man gave me another eight millimetres of teeth.

'I could use some humour this afternoon, Mr Faraday,' he said. 'I guess you pass the test all right. But no funny business.'

'I'm all out of fun today,' I said.

I stood back while he cautiously unlatched the door. He pulled it back and stood in the shadow behind it. His eyes anxiously surveyed the dripping desolation of the landscape.

'You got a name?' I said.

He cleared his throat nervously.

'Call me Bertram.'

I shook my head.

'You don't look like a Bertram to me.'

The thin man locked and bolted the door savagely, his thin, antennae-like fingers trembling. He kept his right hand in his jacket pocket. Now that we were in the off-white hall of the house I could see that he had sleek black hair and a slight scar on one side of his face. He was about forty-five, I should have said, going on seventy; he had one of those emaciated ruins of faces that add about thirty years to the owner's age.

His heavily-padded executive suit didn't disguise his concave chest. Altogether he looked like a 1920s TB patient looking for a place to die. I guess that was unkind but that was the sort of image he conjured up. And the fact that TB has been more or less eradicated today robbed it of any offence. Not that I voiced my thoughts aloud, of course. He moved across the hall, gesturing with his left hand.

'In here, Mr Faraday. You'd like a drink after your drive?'

'I don't usually indulge in the afternoons,' I said. 'But on account of the heavy moisture content of the air today I'm willing to make an exception.'

The thin man flung open a door at the end of the corridor and ushered me through. It was a biggish room with an electric fire featuring phoney logs burning sluggishly in the stone fireplace. The apartment was fitted-up with rumpled, anonymous-looking furniture but what killed it for me was a flight of plaster ducks planing up into the ceiling. They looked like I felt this afternoon.

I sat down on the end of a divan halfway between the centre of the room and the fireplace while the thin man went over to a drinks cabinet in the far corner.

'Bourbon and water all right?' he said.

'Fine,' I said. 'You can go easy on the water, though.'

He bared his teeth briefly again like he'd got the joke. I looked around while he splashed about with glasses and ice. The room gave on to the garden at the back of the house; that was a green, ruined wilderness too and we seemed more at the bottom of the sea than ever. The thin man was silent as he made the drinks; he had on a suit that I thought had gone out with thirties movies. Thick blue and white pin-stripe that made him look like an extra in a Damon Runyon piece.

But I guess it suited his narrow face. He came back over and handed me the drink in a crystal glass. It was about the most expensive thing in the room. I guessed then that the bungalow was a rented one. There was a briefcase lying on a chair by the door and a raincoat and a cigarette lighter on the far end of the divan on which I was sitting.

The thin man toasted me over the rim of his glass.

'Your health, Mr Faraday.'

'I won't argue with that,' I said.

I took my first sip of the drink. It wasn't half bad. I looked round the empty room again.

'Going somewhere?' I said.

'Maybe,' the thin man said defensively.

He put his glass down on a small occasional table in the middle of the room and sat nervously on the arm of a padded chair just beyond it. He looked at me with heavy-lidded eyes.

'I have some information that might be worth your while, Mr Faraday.'

I nodded, taking another sip of my drink. The effect of the weather was wearing off by the minute.

'So you said. I'm listening.'

The thin man put up his hand.

'Not so fast, Mr Faraday. We got to talk money.'

I grinned.

'Mr Zangwill's a rich man, if that's what you mean. I'd have to see what you've got to sell first.'

The thin man looked worried. He stood up abruptly, his icy-grey eyes flickering apprehensively.

'I haven't got the stuff here, Mr Faraday. I'm not that stupid.'

I shook my head.

'No-one's suggested it.'

The thin man stood deep in thought, his head on one side like he was listening for something in the heavy silence. Then he turned to me, his eyes glittering, his fingers shaking visibly.

'What I've got's worth half a million dollars of Mr Zangwill's money,' he said thickly. 'He can well afford it.'

'That's very interesting,' I said. 'That's the second time that sum's been mentioned in the case. I've no doubt Mr Zangwill can afford it. You'll have to have something fantastic to make it worth that much.'

Bertram sat down again, like someone had cut the strings of a marionette. His voice was faint and far away so that I had to strain to hear it.

'It's worth it, Mr Faraday, I can assure you.'

I stared at him thoughtfully.

'You haven't by any chance been hanging around the estate?'

'From time to time,' the thin man said guardedly.

I put my drink down on the small table, my eyes holding his.

'You didn't write any notes to Mr Zangwill? Or exchange shots with his guard?'

Bertram went white, his eyes fixed on mine like a snake transfixing its victim. It didn't work with me but that was the effect he intended. He passed a withered tongue across his blue lips.

'I don't know what you mean, Mr Faraday. I'm in business for myself.'

'Don't you?' I said. 'And you didn't attack Zangwill's secretary by any chance?'

The thin man was alarmed now. He gulped at his drink like it would give him courage. He stood up again, his thin legs trembling like a stork's. A lot of similes were coming to my mind this afternoon but that was the effect he was having on me.

'Look, Mr Faraday, would it do any good if I said I didn't know what you were talking about?'

'It might,' I said. 'Convince me.'

The thin man shook his head.

'I don't have to convince you, Mr Faraday. I can produce the stuff within a couple of days.'

'All right,' I said. 'We can talk again then.'

The thin man swirled the residue of his drink around in his glass, his eyes down on the carpet.

'Of course, Mr Zangwill will have to be present and know what this is all about,' I said.

He held up his hand again, his voice high and thin.

'Mr Zangwill's not in this, Mr Faraday. There'll be no meeting. I'll trade through you or the deal's off. I could send the stuff to the newspapers. Mr Zangwill wouldn't like that.'

I stared at him for a long moment.

'That's interesting,' I said. 'Let's see if I've got this straight. You've something on Zangwill that will blow the roof off if it's released. It's worth half a million to the old man to suppress it. Otherwise he will be ruined if you give it to the media? Am I right?'

The thin man swallowed and gulped the remainder of his drink. He reached out for the bottle again.

'That's basically correct, Mr Faraday.'

I held out my glass for a re-fill. The thin man in the pin-stripe suit poured the whisky and topped it with ice. He was trembling so hard he took twice as long as he should have. I looked at him searchingly.

'You're not cut out for blackmail,' I said. 'Your nerves won't take the strain.'

He sat upright, a dull patch spreading on both his cheeks.

'Blackmail's an ugly word, Mr Faraday.'

'It's an ugly business, Mr Bertram,' I said. 'There's no other way to describe it.'

I put my glass down on the table.

'So how are we going to slice this? I must have something to convince Zangwill that you're on the level. Leastways, as on the level as a blackmailer can be.'

The glass clinked against Bertram's teeth, he was shaking so much as he downed his drink.

'I'm thinking about it, Mr Faraday.'

His eyes had gone hard and suspicious

again. I leaned forward to pick up my drink when the thin man stood up abruptly. A big cannon had suddenly appeared from his pocket. He held it none too steadily on my gut.

'Even I couldn't miss at this range, Mr Faraday.'

I stared at him over the rim of my glass.

'I should be careful if I were you, Mr Bertram. That thing might go off and then we should both be in a mess.'

He shrugged. I looked at the cannon. The safety was off all right.

'For Christ's sake point it at the floor,' I said. 'That way we'll both be safer.'

'As soon as you unship yours,' he said. 'I saw the bulge just now.'

I stared at him.

'Your reflexes are like greased molasses,' I said. 'If I'd meant you any harm you'd have been taken out half an hour ago.'

The thin man looked sullen. His lower lip quivered. For one second I thought he was going to cry.

'Nevertheless, Mr Faraday, I'd feel safer if you didn't have it. Just stand up slowly and take it out the holster nice and slow. Then drop it on the floor.'

I got up and reached slowly in my jacket. There didn't seem any reason not to, and at least one why I should. He could have put a hole as big as a freeway tunnel through me in a split-second and I'm the sort of character who doesn't look good with two navels. I did like he said.

CHAPTER SEVEN

1

The Smith-Wesson hit the carpet with a thump and the thin man kicked it over toward the far window. It hit the skirting with a faint crack. He had a smile on his face now. He went and sat back on the arm of the chair and put the gun carefully on the seat. I felt better then. I sat down too and picked up my drink.

'Now what?' I said.

Bertram shook his head.

'I'm thinking, Mr Faraday. I want this all sorted out within two days.'

'You'll be lucky,' I said.

The thin man blinked like he was coming out of a long sleep.

'You don't understand, Mr Faraday. I'm tired. I got to make a quick killing and get out. Out of the state with enough to last me for the rest of my life.'

I slipped my second glass, savouring the smoky taste of the liquor on my tongue.

'Killing is right, Mr Bertram. You're in a very dangerous business. Blackmailers don't usually meet with happy endings.'

The thin man shivered suddenly, his narrowed eyes staring out at the sodden wilderness of the garden beyond the windows. He gave a heavy sigh.

'That's what my friends tell me, Mr Faraday. But I've got a chance here. The biggest of my life and I mean to take it.'

'It's your life,' I said. 'What's your suggestion?'

The thin man looked at me cunningly.

'No, tricks, Mr Faraday. Or this thing blows wide open. And it's no use coming back here. I won't be around.'

I shook my head, swilling the bourbon and the ice around in my glass with a faint chinking noise.

'Straight down the line,' I said. 'You'd better fix a new meeting place. And bring a sample of the goods for sale.'

He kept his eyes down so it was difficult to read his face.

'What is it?' I said. 'Letters?'

Bertram shook his head.

'Photographs, Mr Faraday. There's no harm in telling you that. If they were published it would be the biggest scandal since the South Sea Bubble.'

'Interesting,' I said.

He cleared his throat with an ugly rasping noise.

'You'd think so. I can't be more specific, though I'd like to be. And I can't overemphasize that when next we meet and I hand over a sample print, copies will still be in a safe place.'

'Like a train station locker,' I said.

He smiled faintly, little patches of red standing out on his cheeks.

'Maybe, Mr Faraday,' he said softly.

'How did you get hold of these pictures?' I said.

He shook his head vigorously.

'That's restricted information. You're asking too many questions.'

'It always was one of my failings,' I said.

I looked over toward the window. The Smith-Wesson lay with its muzzle just resting against the skirting board. Not that I intended to try anything with Bertram in his present state of nerves. It was for information only. I turned back toward the thin man. He lookcd a crushed and defeated character who had one overriding ambition: to squeeze Zangwill until the pips ran dry. I wondered what pictures he could have which would be worth so much. And whether he had worked for the old man at one time.

It would be almost impossible to identify him. Zangwill must have had thousands of people on his payroll at various periods. I didn't figure Bertram for a mining character but Zangwill must have had thousands on his clerical and administrative staffs too. Anyway, it would be something for me to check on later. I wouldn't tell the old man anything about this development for the time being.

Leastways, not in detail. I didn't want to tip my hand and if there was anything in his past he hadn't told me about, I might catch him off guard some time. In my experience clients who were being blackmailed—and I'd had quite a few—were always less than forthcoming about their own pasts. Not surprisingly, of course, but it didn't make my job any easier.

I looked up. Bertram had risen from his chair like he'd come to a decision.

'I just thought of something, Mr Faraday. Something that would suit both our purposes.'

'I'm glad of that,' I said. 'I was hoping we weren't going to sit here all day.'

'We'll meet tomorrow if that's convenient to you,' Bertram said. 'Like I said I'll bring one print. That should be enough to convince you—and the old man.'

'All right,' I said.

I drained the rest of the whisky in my glass. I was dry enough now and though I hadn't taken off my raincoat I felt comfortable enough because the house had a chill, unlived in feeling. I wondered then if Bertram had borrowed it just for one afternoon. Something strange about him drew my attention. He'd seemed a little uneasy the past few minutes.

Now he held up his hand to enjoin silence. The pistol had grown back into his right fist.

'What's the matter?' I said.

Bertram's lips showed as a thin, white line.

'I thought I heard a car a minute or two ago,' he said.

'So what?' I said. 'One of the neighbours, perhaps.'

He shook his head.

'You miss the point, Mr Faraday. I chose this place carefully. There's no-one in the houses round about. They're used only in the season or up for sale. The other occupants commute to the city. They don't get back until around half-six. There's something I don't like about this.'

His face hardened in suspicion, his finger tightening on the trigger of the cannon.

'You didn't bring anyone with you?'

'Talk sense,' I said. 'What would be the point?'

We were standing like that when the window to the garden smashed inward and two, black circular objects rolled into the centre of the room. I threw myself toward the garden end of the apartment as tongues of flame licked outward, scorched my face. I didn't hear the explosions but felt myself floating toward the ceiling in a shower of sparks and disintegrating fragments.

2

I tasted blood as I came down. My hands were burned and I sucked air into my aching lungs. Someone was screaming from far away but I had no time to take any notice. The Smith-Wesson was in my hand now but I had no target. The room was a white-hot mass of flame that seemed to grow every second. I threw myself out through the shattered panes into the friendly moisture of the garden. Even the glass was hot, the fire had been so quick in spreading.

I knew what had caused it but it would have to wait; my brain wasn't working properly for the moment. I landed heavily, winded myself. I felt refreshing rain on my face, rolled over in wet grass. Choking black smoke was rolling out the window casement.

The screaming had stopped now. I knew it was too late for Bertram. Whoever wanted to shut his mouth had done a good job. If he hadn't disarmed me I might have done something about it. But I knew even as the idea flickered across my brain that nothing would have been very effective against the things that had been lobbed in.

I got away down the garden into the shelter of some trees. I was just in time. There was another big explosion then and window glass sprayed about the lawn in thousands of miniature darts. Either there had been a quick build-up of fumes inside or the fire had got to a gas main. Either way there was no point in me hanging around to be identified. The people in the houses round about must be either deaf or asleep.

Then I remembered what Bertram had just said. It seemed like years ago but it couldn't have been more than thirty seconds. The whole of the bungalow was aflame now and the roof caved in as I watched, sending great plumes of white and orange smoke to mix with the rain in hissing clouds of steam. There weren't many people up here to be alarmed by the explosions.

And in any event anyone sitting indoors in a house only a hundred yards off might not even have heard them above the noises of the wind and the rain. It all depended on the direction of the wind. And thirty seconds wasn't long measured in terms of reaction time.

I heard a car gun up then, found the cogs of my brain working. I pounded across the grass, threw myself at a tangled hedge. I was in a neighbouring garden and I got down the zig-zag concrete path in such good time that I must have looked like a clip from an old Olympic Games film. It wasn't any good though. The anonymous-looking dark sedan was already snaking along the road, halfway down the bluff.

I pounded up toward the Buick, remembered then that it was facing the wrong way. I decided not to bother. I'd never catch him on these roads and in these weather conditions. I'd heard the whine of a supercharger and I knew my old Buick was no match for such a souped-up vehicle. That was why it had been used, obviously.

Incredibly, no-one and nothing had moved in all the expanse of the road, though black smoke was soaring skywards.

I got back to the Buick, trying to walk normally, feeling like I was on a lighted stage. I felt guilty about not reporting the outbreak to the fire department but there was nothing anyone could have done. The building was already burned halfway to the ground and the fire hadn't been going more than a minute. The special bombs the unknown man had thrown in had generated terrific heat and if I knew anything about it such a fire couldn't have been stopped without special equipment.

I had a good idea what the bombs were but I'd get to that later. It was obvious now that I wouldn't be getting any photographs that might throw light on Zangwill's past. Unless Bertram had an accomplice, of course. I'd just have to sit tight for a day or two and see what happened. I was swearing to myself as I got up to my heap. My only lead had literally vanished in a puff of smoke just as I was getting somewhere.

I found I was still holding the Smith-Wesson in my right hand. I'd have been arrested on sight had there been a cop around. I put it back in the holster, aware that I was drenched with rain. Another part of the bungalow roof went then and I could hear a car coming up the bluff. I remembered the narrowness of the roads and a sense of preservation galvanized me into action.

I got behind the wheel quickly, turned round as unobtrusively as possible in the circular space built for that purpose. I trundled back down the road as slowly as I dared, watching the big cone of red fire in my rear-mirror, until a bend in the road blotted it out. But I could still see the smoke ascending for another mile.

I looked at myself in the mirror. I looked a wreck. My face was streaked with smoke; my hair hung lank and saturated over my forehead; and my reddened eyes were weeping tears. I would have been just the thing for the hero of a Fannie Hurst movie if they still made such things. I drove with one hand and reached for my handkerchief. I tried to make myself presentable while my right hand did its best to keep the automobile on the road.

I got over a mile away before the first cars started coming up. I was hunched down but the drivers had no time for me. They pressed on round the bend and I had the road to myself. I waited until I got on to a decent piece of tarmac. Then I put my toe down and started making time back in to the city.

CHAPTER EIGHT

1

It was still raining when I got there. I parked the car, walked a couple of blocks and used a pay-phone. I dialled Stella's home number but there was no reply. I looked at my watch but it was only just coming up to six so she wouldn't have been back yet anyway. I tried the office number but there was no reply there either. She was obviously on her way so I drove to her apartment block.

I sat in the Buick, tidied myself as best I could and smoked a cigarette while I waited. The rain drummed monotonously on the hood and sluiced down the storm-drains. I was in the private parking lot belonging to the apartments so there weren't many other vehicles around.

It was around half-past six before she showed. I let her park and walk into the building before I followed. I caught her in the lobby as she was buttoning the elevator. There was slight shock in her eyes as she stared at me. Fortunately there was no-one else around at this precise moment.

'You look as if you'd seen a ghost, Mike.'

I nodded grimly.

'That's about it, honey. Can I come up? I'd like the benefit of your advice.'

'Sure.'

We got in the elevator cage and glided upward. We were both silent until she put the key in the door of her apartment. I followed her in and closed it behind me.

Stella stood shaking droplets of moisture off her raincoat, her eyes searching my face. Now that we were in the brighter light of the apartment she took in the details as I took off my trenchcoat. She hung hers up on a hanger in a cupboard and deftly slipped one through my own.

'You look as though you've been stoking a bonfire, Mike.'

'That's just about it,' I said. 'Mind if I wash-up?'

Stella went swiftly across the living room.

'I'll make something to eat. You know where the bathroom is.'

'I remember,' I said.

I avoided looking in the mirror when I got in there. When I'd finished and combed my hair I felt I might live with a little care and kindness. There was an agreeable aroma coming from the kitchen when I got back there. Stella was standing by the stainless steel draining board chopping up vegetables with a very sharp knife on a wooden board. She wore

87

a blue and white striped apron and she looked great, like always.

'Have a glass of white wine.'

'Why not?' I said. 'I've already had two glasses of whisky. And been to a cremation.'

Stella's hand trembled on the handle of the knife and she put it down on the block with a clatter.

'I think I'll have a drink myself, Mike. You'll find some glasses over there.'

I got the bottle out the refrigerator and did like she said. We drank in silence. Stella's face was white beneath the tan.

'You're talking about the man who phoned you this morning?'

I nodded.

He was a blackmailer trying to shake Zangwill down. Someone got to him before we could get to the meat.'

Stella took her glass from the draining board and carried it out in the living room. She sat down in a big chair one side of the stone fireplace. She held the glass carefully between the fingers of both hands and stared at it like she was concentrating her thoughts.

'So we got a mess, Mike?'

I sat down opposite her and studied her face.

'Looks like it,' I said. 'The little man was called Bertram. I gathered that was his surname, not his Christian name. It was obviously assumed, anyway.'

I went on to tell Stella what had happened. She listened in silence, occasionally taking a sip at the wine. The colour was coming back to her cheeks now. I leaned back in my chair when I finished. I was getting hoarse with talking.

'Any suggestions gratefully received,' I said.

'Strange both these sets of people mentioned half a million dollars. Assuming two different sets are involved.'

I frowned at her over the rim of my glass.

'I believed him. So would you if you'd been there. I figure he was working on his own.'

'So the people who sent those notes might have taken him out?' said Stella dubiously. 'But surely they wouldn't have been peddling the same material?'

I grinned.

'I didn't say the case was easy, honey.'

Stella smiled too. She sat up in the chair, tucking her feet beneath her. She still wore the striped apron.

'Perhaps we'll get a bulletin on the radio,' she said, looking at her watch.

'Let it wait,' I said. 'They won't have anything at this early stage we don't already know. I'd still like the benefit of your thoughts.'

'I've been waiting for this day a long time,' Stella told the wallpaper.

She put her empty glass down on a low teak table next her chair.

'You were lucky to get out, Mike.'

'You can say that again,' I said. 'Those bombs were of the jelly type. They start the sort of fire you can't stop.'

'Meaning what?" Stella said.

I shrugged.

'They were a special type of hand grenade. The sort of thing they used in the Vietnam War.'

Stella shivered slightly like it was cold in here. She got up abruptly.

'We'll think better with some food inside us, Mike.'

2

I lit my third cigarette and pulled my second cup of coffee over toward me. Like always, the food had been great. We were back in the living room again now; Stella sat opposite me, her face thoughtful and abstracted.

'Zangwill hasn't exactly been frank with you, Mike.'

'You can say that again,' I said. 'He's a strange sort of man altogether.'

Stella shifted slightly in her chair.

'But you thought he was on the level?'

'He impressed me as being that way,' I said. 'It wouldn't be the first time I had a client who was less than forthcoming.'

Stella cupped her hands over her right

knee-cap and frowned at the pattern in the carpet.

'Zangwill's past seems quite open and shut, Mike.'

'From the public record,' I said. 'Who knows, from the personal point of view. So far as I could make out he's in the clear from the moral angle. There were no women, drink or drug problems. From what Laura Billington says he lived only for his wife. After that there was only his business, which he conducted at long distance.'

'So we have to look there for a blackmail motive,' Stella said.

'Maybe,' I said. 'I told the girl the case was impossible for me to handle without any further data. She's having a talk with the old man and I'm expecting to get something when I see him tomorrow. If I see him tomorrow.'

Stella smiled faintly.

'You see him tomorrow,' she said. 'I fixed another appointment. The old man wasn't very pleased, according to Miss Billington. Apparently he's not used to being stood up.'

I blew a feather of blue smoke up toward the ceiling of the apartment.

'That's a surprise too.' I said. 'From what the girl said he's had no appointments over which to be stood up for years.'

Stella's eyes were very frank and bright.

'Maybe things are changing, Mike.'

'Meaning what?' I said.

She shrugged.

'Perhaps he wanted to be open with you. He'd screwed himself up to the point of being frank about his private life. Then he felt let down at not being able to see you today.'

I stared at her.

'It's possible,' I said. 'Anything's possible. But it's pretty thin stuff. If you'd seen the old man . . .'

I tipped the ash off my cigarette into an elegant crystal tray on Stella's table.

'According to the girl he'd been frightened out of his life over these notes. But either he's a very good actor or he has remarkable powers of recovery. He looked pretty normal to me when we talked.'

Stella got up from her chair with a quick, lithe movement. She came over and poured me another coffee from the silver pot on the tray on the table.

'It hardly matters now, Mike. You'll be hearing about it at firsthand tomorrow. I fixed another appointment for three o'clock. Afternoon suits him best.'

'Fine,' I said. 'He'll have to do better than last time if I'm going to take it any further.'

Stella sat down again, her eyes restless and penetrating.

'What are you going to tell him about this business out at the bungalow?'

I shook my head.

'Precisely nothing. Leastways, not for a

while. I'll let him make the running. I'll maybe nose about the estate tomorrow, question some of the staff. Something may surface.'

I focused my gaze up on to Stella's elegant rococo-style ceiling. It made a change from that at the office.

'The maddening thing is that this set of pictures is probably gathering dust somewhere in a public locker in the L.A. area.'

Stella put her pink fingers together in her lap. The gold bell of her hair shimmered under the lamps.

'It wouldn't be any good sifting through the wreckage of the house?'

I shook my head.

'You weren't there, honey. There wouldn't be anything to sift, assuming I could have got there. The fire people, the police and the insurance boys will be over it with a fine-tooth comb. They'll probably work throughout tonight. I doubt if there would be anything to find but fine ash and fused metal.'

Stella nodded slowly.

'The interesting thing will be when someone clears the locker. If Zangwill has anything in his past to hide, it's bound to come out.'

I stared at her for a, long moment. That was something I hadn't thought of.

'Good reasoning,' I said. 'Depends whether there's anything to identify the prints. Stuff in public lockers usually goes to Lost or Unclaimed Property. It's got to be pretty dynamic to get to the police.'

I stubbed out my cigarette in the tray.

'Unless the character who lobbed those bombs in knew where the stuff was stashed.'

'There's a nice lot of questions to be going on with,' said Stella brightly.

I looked at her sharply but I couldn't detect any irony on her face. But then I never can. I gave up beating my brains out. There'd be enough problems to hold over until tomorow. Like they say, tomorrow is another day.

CHAPTER NINE

1

It was ten of three when I hit Zangwill's again. It was still raining. So far as I was concerned it would still be raining when the case ended and for months afterward. If it ever ended. If it ever started, come to that. I grinned faintly as I drew the Buick to a stop near the entrance to Zangwill's place.

There was something else crazy about the set-up. My appointments so far had all been at three o'clock in the afternoon. And this was the third since I'd started. On the third day too. I bared my teeth at my image in the rear mirror. It's a good job you're not superstitious, Mike, I told myself.

There was something different out here today, though. The first thing was that the chain across, the main entrance drive had been removed. I could see it lying on the ground. For a second or two I felt an odd sensation in the pit of my stomach; it's like the sort of thing you feel when sudden disaster hits. It lasted only a moment because someone came running out through the small white wicket gate.

It wasn't Kempton this time but a young, blond-haired guard in the smart grey uniform of a security firm. He wore a yellow slicker over it and there was a waterproof cover of the same colour over his stiff peaked cap. He sprinted toward me as I wound the window down.

'Miss Billington said you were to drive straight on up today, Mr Faraday.'

'Fine,' I said. 'What happened to Kempton?'

'He has a couple of days off,' the young man said. 'I deputize for him most times.'

'Right,' I said. 'Don't get wet.'

I hadn't killed the motor so I let in the gear, reversed a few yards and turned into the driveway. In the rear mirror I could see the young fellow hooking the chain back across the gateway. There was no sign of the dog. Then I remembered it would be a one-man, one-dog setup. I hoped Kempton had taken it with him, wherever he'd gone on his off-duty break.

I pulled the Buick up in front of the vast porch and got quickly over toward the front door. It was only a few yards but already I was soaking wet. I hoped the rest of the case would take place indoors. I grinned to myself. Maybe the case would be discontinued because it was too wet. It wasn't a very funny joke really but I had to make my own amusements and it was all I had this afternoon.

I rang the brass bellpush for the second time and listened to its pealing away inside the house. It seemed like years since I had last been up here. I thought again of Zangwill's lonely life until the girl came and that haunted mausoleum at the edge of the lake. I wouldn't have lived here under those circumstances for all of Zangwill's money. This time there was no hesitation; I heard the quick, eager footsteps almost before the bell had stopped ringing.

Once again it was the girl who opened the door to me. Today she wore a classically modelled white sweater with a roll neck and a tiny gold ornament glistened at her breast. Her slim grey skirt had the deceptive simplicity of expensive tailoring. Her violet eyes looked smoky and enigmatic in the dim light of the porch.

'I thought we'd break the rules for once and let you drive up to save you getting wet.'

'I'm all for that, Laura,' I said. 'Breaking rules I mean.'

She smiled faintly, holding the door wide for me to pass through.

'We'd better go to the study first. I want to talk to you before you see Mr Zangwill.'

'You mean to say he isn't hiding in the gallery,' I said.

Her eyes were difficult to read when she turned to me as we crossed the hall.

'This is serious, Mike. Mr Zangwill was all ready to talk to you yesterday. Today, I'm not so sure.'

'Then he was holding something back?' I said.

The girl pressed her lips together in a thin line.

'You might say so. He's a difficult man, like I said. I'd like to explain that too.'

'All right,' I said. 'If I get much more of this tea ritual I'll be spoiled for the gritty end of the P.I. business.'

Laura Billington smiled, revealing again the perfect teeth. We were in the study now and I saw that Mrs Meakins was already pouring at the small table before the log fire.

'You must have electronic timing to be this precise,' I said.

Mrs Meakins gave me a severe smile.

'The young man in the lodge buzzed as soon as your vehicle appeared, Mr Faraday. That gave me time to finish making the tea. It's very important to get the proper blend and flavour.'

'I'll take your word for it,' I said.

'Incidentally, I'd like to talk to you later if Miss Billington has no objection.'

The housekeeper masked her surprise well. Her teeth caught at her lower lip and she glanced quickly at the girl. Laura Billington dropped casually into her chair.

'Of course there's no objection,' she said softly. 'Mrs Meakins' room is the next door beyond this one. You might like to see her after we finish up here as I've no idea how long Mr Zangwill will be.'

I took off my raincoat, put it on the back of my armchair and sat down opposite the girl.

'Is he tied up this afternoon?' I said.

Another strange glance passed between the two women. Then Mrs Meakins said softly, 'I am at your disposal, Mr Faraday.'

She went out, walking with firm, decisive steps, and closed the door quietly behind her. The girl made a great display of cheerfulness, holding out a plate of toast to me.

'Let's hope we shall be more successful today, Mr Faraday, than we were on the last occasion.'

I lifted my cup to my lips.

'I'll drink to that,' I said.

2

The girl's finely moulded face looked guileless in the firelight, the soft brown hair masking it so thickly it seemed like it was to conceal it from the intrusive gaze of strangers. She sat watching me in silence for a couple of minutes. Then she seemed to come to a decision.

'Your secretary hinted at some development in Mr Zangwill's case yesterday.'

I nodded.

'You could call it a development. If you could call it a case.'

The girl gave a faint sigh, stretching herself in the armchair like a cat.

'I hope we're not going to get bogged down in all that again, Mike.'

I shook my head.

'Not today. It was put to me by the party who approached me that Mr Zangwill had something in his past that might leave him open to blackmail. Does that ring a bell?'

There was genuine shock on the girl's face now. She opened her mouth as though to speak, then bit back the words. The violet eyes were clouded again.

'There are things in most men's lives that leave them vulnerable and open to misinterpretation.'

'That sounds like the loyal secretary speaking, Laura,' I said.

The girl flinched like I'd struck her. Her jaw tightened. It was the first time I'd really noticed how firm and square it was.

'It also sounds like the normal reaction of any thinking human being,' she said softly.

'You have a point,' I told her. 'The thing is, I've been operating in the dark ever since I came through this door. I'd like something tangible from you or Mr Zangwill today that will give me some teeth for the sort of operation that will let him come out covered with roses.'

The girl was smiling a tight smile through clenched teeth. It didn't make her look any less attractive.

'I'm not sure I like your simile, Mike. It sounds almost funereal to me.'

I nodded grimly.

'It was almost funereal to me.'

The girl's lips trembled slightly as her troubled eyes searched my face.

'You wouldn't care to put it a little more plainly.'

I shook my head.

'Not until I know what I'm getting into. But a man was killed yesterday when he contacted me over this business.'

Again, the shock and puzzlement in the girl's features was genuine. Or else she was the finest actress in the world.

'You can't be serious.'

'I was never more serious,' I said. 'So you can see why I want some facts. And I need them fast.'

Laura Billington seemed to have been frozen by some tremendous inner force.

'This information mustn't get to Mr

Zangwill,' she said sharply. 'At least, not at this early stage.'

'Exactly my sentiments,' I said. 'I was going to ask for your silence, but I can see it wouldn't have been necessary.'

The secretary shook the brown hair round her face, little sparks of anger dancing in her eyes.

'The sort of thing you've just told me would be enough to kill him in his present frame of mind.'

My eyes held hers briefly before she turned away.

'So you keep saying. Yet he seems a remarkably robust and self-contained old man to me.'

The girl was angry now but she held herself under control. Her breasts rose and fell deeply beneath the thick white sweater.

'There are a lot of things I could say in reply, Mr Faraday, but I'll confine myself to a few general remarks. You don't know him like I've known him over the past few years. He has a public facade and a private persona, like most people. The two are very different.'

She looked at me fiercely, her eyes a smoky blue.

'Believe me he's a childish, frightened, lonely old man for ninety-per-cent of the time. It's only my restoration of his business and book-writing interests that maintain his precarious hold on life at all.'

She had the faintest smile at the corners of her mouth now as I continued to stare at her.

'All right,' I said. 'Point taken. Believe me too. I'm not just being awkward about this. I almost got killed yesterday. I want to know what I'm getting into. If there's anything in Zangwill's past that will make sense of this business then I've a right to know it. A man who wanted to give me information is dead. I'm at a dead end too if you or the old man can't come up with something.'

The girl nodded, all the animosity and anger dying out of her. She clasped her hands together until white skin showed on her knuckles.

'Very well, Mike. As you say. We'll just quietly finish our tea. Then you have your talk with Mrs Meakins. While you're doing that I'll go up to see Mr Zangwill. He does appreciate your problems but I'll underline the difficulties you're having. I will say nothing of what you've told me, of course. Before you leave here we'll have something concrete for you to go on, one way or another.'

I stared at her for a long moment.

'Let's hope so,' I said.

CHAPTER TEN

1

Mrs Meakins was sitting bolt upright in a big wing-chair in her room sipping tea too when I got to see her. I was beginning to feel that I didn't want to see another cucumber sandwich as long as I lived. Maybe that was a little uncharitable. It was probably the surroundings and the frustrating circumstances of the old man's case.

Something of the sternness had dropped away from the housekeeper's attitude and I sensed an apprehension in her eyes as she waved me into another big chair opposite. I seemed to have been living through scenes from *Pride and Prejudice* the last few days. If one excepted the décor at Bertram's bungalow, that is. Even that was beginning to seem as remote as a dream.

Before I could speak Mrs Meakins forestalled me.

'I think I should warn you, sir, that I cannot say anything against the family. And if your questions should open up a certain line of inquiry I may have to refuse to answer.

She looked at me defiantly.

'I would rather do that than lie to you. Or anyone else,' she concluded after a few seconds.

I stared at her in surprise.

'I'm not looking for lies, Mrs Meakins. But you do realize that your remarks reveal a rather peculiar state of affairs out here. I'm working to further Mr Zangwill's interests, you understand.'

The housekeeper lowered the cup from her lips and replaced it in the saucer, a faint smile on her heavy features beneath the grey hair. She looked like an old still from *Rebecca* as she did so. It only needed George Sanders at the window. But this wasn't the day for it and George wouldn't be around any more, unfortunately.

'I fully understand that, sir. But I felt I had to make my own position clear.'

I leaned back in my chair and studied her thoughtfully.

'Just what is your position, Mrs Meakins?'

She was fully in control of herself now.

'Nothing more than that of a loyal employee, Mr Faraday.'

'But if the truth clashed with Mr Zangwill's interests, you'd bend the truth?' I said.

She shook her head, her eyes somewhere far away.

'I wouldn't have put it exactly like that, sir.'

It was another big, dark room we were in; no-one up here seemed to bother about switching on lights during the day and the eerie green jungle with which the house was surrounded, made everything swim in an aqueous twilight. There was a sort of bureau beyond where she sat that was crowded with photographs; large portraits, views; shots, of the house in which we were sitting; and stiffly posed groups, possibly staff photographs of Zangwill and his employees.

There might be something interesting there if I could find an excuse to go on over before the interview was over. It hadn't started very promisingly, though, and I didn't hold out much hope. I needed Stella at my elbow to prompt my wits. They seemed to slow down in the old-world atmosphere out here. Mrs Meakins was looking at me rather maliciously it seemed. Or maybe it was just the lighting.

'I don't want to give you the wrong impression, Mr Faraday,' she said after a stiff silence. 'I'm perfectly happy to co-operate. It's just that I'd like to avoid certain areas of confidence.'

I looked at her sharply.

'Such as?'

She shifted uncomfortably in her chair.

'If the questions got too personal. About the family, I mean.'

I shook my head.

'I wouldn't ask you to betray a trust, Mrs Meakins. You should know that.'

The housekeeper's manner relaxed slightly. She gave me a curt inclination of her head like I'd just been admitted to her confidence.

'How much do you know of this business?'

The eyebrows were raised now until it seemed to me in the dimness of the room that they were in danger of meeting the dusty grey hair.

'What business, Mr Faraday?'

I looked at her in exasperation.

'You mean you got more than one mystery around here?'

Mrs Meakins flushed. I'd struck home there all right.

'Forgive me, sir. You're correct, of course. That was a foolish response to your question. You mean the threats against Mr Zangwill's life and the demand for that huge sum of money.'

I held out my package of cigarettes. The grey-haired woman shook her head. She looked like an old print of Queen Victoria sitting there in the semi-darkness.

'I don't smoke, Mr Faraday. I regard it as a disgusting habit. But go ahead if you must.'

I grinned and put the package back in my pocket.

'The hell with it. I'd hate to spoil the atmosphere of your room. I'm still waiting for your answer.'

The severe-looking woman shrugged.

'I'm not paid to meditate on Mr Zangwill's private affairs or on his business interests, sir. I'm merely paid to look after the house and his personal comforts.'

'It's an admirablc attitude,' I said. 'But you must have formed some theories about this matter.'

The eyes were regarding me shrewdly now.

'Perhaps someone with a grudge from Mr Zangwill's business life. A gentleman of his wide-ranging interests must have formed some enemies during his long career in the metal-mining industry.'

'That's a little better,' I said. 'But you wouldn't be able to direct me to any specific areas?'

I thought there was a slight hesitation in the housekeeper's eyes. They flickered over my shoulder. I became aware that the room door had opened silently in the gloom. I turned. The girl was standing there, like an insubstantial shadow.

'I'm sorry, Mr Faraday. I didn't want to disturb you but Mr Zangwill is asking for Mrs Meakins rather urgently. Something has come up. He won't keep her more than two minutes.'

'Sure,' I said.

I got up. The housekeeper got up hurriedly too, brushing down her skirts like they were covered with crumbs.

She gave me a distant bow.

'Excuse me, Mr Faraday.'

She went out hurriedly and I could hear her and the girl whispering softly in the doorway. Then the door closed and the footsteps went away. It suited me fine. I went over close to where the photographs were ranged. I went through them quickly, looking at the fading, blank faces.

There was one of Zangwill and a striking-looking woman who held the bridle of a horse. Obviously his wife; there were groups of people in the grounds, posed stiffly, eyes a little glazed, wary of the camera. In most of them Zangwill, looking a good deal younger, was sitting on a chair in the centre, with most of the people standing behind him. I guessed they were staff photographs of the people on the estate.

There was one which particularly interested me; it had Zangwill sitting in the centre as usual, with the girl seated to his left; there was a dark-haired man in his mid-thirties on the old man's right, with Mrs Meakins standing rather deferentially behind Zangwill's chair. I went through the figures in the background rather perfunctorily. There were two or three women and four men. I passed them over, came back again.

One suddenly seemed to swim into focus like it was coming out the frame in the manner of a 3-D image. I looked closer. I was slightly smiling as I turned away. One piece at least had just fallen into position. The man staring stiffly into camera was some years younger than I remembered but it was undoubtedly the same person.

Only yesterday he'd been called Bertram and the last time I'd seen him he'd been writhing in agony as the fire got to him out at the bungalow.

2

I was conscious that the housekeeper was back in the room again. She was smiling awkwardly.

'I'm sorry about that, Mr Faraday. It was Mr Zangwill, as you no doubt heard. When we had finished our talk he remarked that he would be able to see you in half an hour or so.'

The eyebrows were raised again; whether interrogatively or disdainfully I couldn't make out.

'He particularly asked me to say that he thought the interview would be more satisfactory for you than that of the other day.'

'Glad to hear it,' I said.

I took her by the arm and drew her over to the group of photographs.

'There's a picture here I'm interested in. Could you run your eyes over it.'

'By all means.'

The grey-haired woman gently but firmly disengaged her arm from mine. She bent toward the wooden-framed photograph I indicated.

'Yes, that was taken some years ago. You'll have recognized myself and Mr Zangwill and

Miss Billington.'

'Of course,' I said. 'It's the other people I'm interested in. Who's the young man in the front row?'

The woman pursed up her lips.

'That's Mr Cameron, Mr Zangwill's nephew. He's an architect in L.A., but we haven't seen him for some time.'

'Mr Zangwill didn't mention him,' I said.

Mrs Meakins smiled faintly.

'When you know Mr Zangwill better—that is, if you're on the case long enough—you'll come to realize he rarely volunteers any gratuitous information.'

I gave her one of my wry looks.

'That's a pity. Because I don't know how I'm going to be able to help him if he doesn't come clean.'

I turned to the picture again.

'Who's the thin man with the scar on the far right in the back row there?'

Mrs Meakins' eyes followed my pointing finger.

'Oh, him.'

There was contempt in the voice.

'He's a man called Bassett. He was Mr Zangwill's chauffeur until a couple of years back.'

I waited for her to continue, but she remained silent.

'Go on,' I said. 'What happened to him?'

She shrugged, re-seating herself in the big

chair.

'Mr Zangwill sacked him. For theft if you must have the precise reason. It was the first time anything like that had happened on the estate.'

She looked a little white now, like she was suppressing her feelings and having some difficulty in doing so.

'Don't get all frayed round the edges,' I said. 'These are the sort of questions that have to be asked.'

The woman's eyes were fixed on me with a wounded look.

'I don't like raking up the past, Mr Faraday,' she snapped. 'It's too painful.'

'It always is,' I said. 'But it's got to be done if I'm to help Mr Zangwill. You should try to remember that.'

There was resentment in the eyes now and then the woman's expression softened.

'Please forgive me, Mr Faraday. I do realize you're trying to help.'

'So long as we understand one another,' I said. 'I'd still like any details you can remember about this business, if you can cast your mind back.'

There was silence for a moment or two as Mrs Meakins sat on in her chair, her eyes blank. I put the photograph down and went over to sit opposite her again.

She stirred herself at last.

'Mr Zangwill's been a worried man as far as

111

I can remember, Mr Faraday.'

'Ever since you came?'

Mrs Meakins nodded.

'Years before that. It's to do with Mrs Zangwill's death long ago. But I expect Miss Billington's told you all that.'

I nodded.

'We've been into it. Doesn't it seem curious to you that it should keep eating at him? I know he was devoted to her but even grief burns itself out. Long before forty years.'

The housekeeper looked at me with an enigmatic expression.

'Maybe, Mr Faraday,' she said softly. 'But you're a young man. If you've known a great love; you've got everything in the world besides, including money and power; and then you get a terrible accident like that, it could knock you sideways.'

She shifted suddenly in the chair, like she was afraid someone might be listening to our conversation.

'And then there's always remorse . . .' she said.

I fixed my eyes sharply on her face.

'What do, you mean by that?'

Mrs Meakins leaned over and switched on a small shaded lamp on a table at her elbow. Her face sprang suddenly out, a white oval floating against the dark material of her easy chair; all the people in the photographs seemed to come to life too. The heads were

112

almost alive; some quizzical; some pensive; some with accusing eyes. The scene seemed to sum up the whole of Zangwill's estate which lay there in the teeming rain, keeping its secrets. It was certainly keeping them from me at any rate.

The housekeeper roused herself at last.

'I think maybe Mr Zangwill blamed himself for the accident, Mr Faraday. That horse had always been high-spirited and dangerous. He constantly warned her about the way she rode it about the grounds.'

'Dangerous rider was she?' I said.

Mrs Meakins shook her head.

'Not dangerous, Mr Faraday. But reckless. She had no thought for herself. There's ravines and bluffs about the grounds. She thought nothing of jumping a wide ravine if the mood was on her. Mr Zangwill always intended to sell the horse but his wife persuaded him not to.'

She looked at me broodingly.

'After, he had the animal put down,' she said slowly. 'After was too late.'

She shivered suddenly, like it had grown cold in the room.

'I'm afraid that's all I can tell you about Mr Zangwill and his affairs, Mr Faraday.'

I got up slowly.

'You've done just fine, Mrs Meakins. You've told me a lot.'

I left her there in the dimness and the

silence, alone with the photographs and her memories. It seemed like a different world once I got outside in the hall.

CHAPTER ELEVEN

1

The girl was sitting in a carved wooden chair the other side the hall like I was a patient visiting a doctor and she was his wife waiting for some doom-laden verdict. I grinned to myself. I guess the atmosphere out here was getting to me as well. Maybe that and the rain. She got up with a quick, nervous movement as I came near.

'I hope Mrs Meakins was able to help, Mike.'

I nodded.

'I got one or two interesting pointers,' I said.

Laura Billington looked at me searchingly.

'We still have a few minutes before Mr Zangwill will be ready. He has his own sitting-room up top, where he works on his books and articles. Let's go on up.'

I nodded and stood aside to let her precede me up the great curving sweep of the staircase. The house was silent and hushed except for the faint sound of the wind and the tapping of the rain at the big oval windows which lit the stairhead. It seemed like I had been living for years like this; almost as though one were struggling for the answers to impossible questions at the bottom of some vast goldfish bowl.

There was a large landing at the top from which seven or eight white-painted doors opened out. The girl chose one halfway down on the right and opened it. It was a big room, with another stone fireplace and books under glass; mostly technical tomes on mining and geology I noticed after we'd been there a short while. There was a modern-looking rosewood desk facing us, in front of the fireplace with its owner's chair set so that his back would catch the warmth of the fire.

There was a low fire burning now and large curved windows at the end of the room gave a sweeping view of the garden under its curtain of rain; I could see tree-tops waving in the wind and there was a fine view of the lake down below, with the whiteness of the mausoleum standing out against the green of the grass and the steel-blue of the water.

'We'll discuss this again after you talk with Mr Zangwill,' the Billington number said. 'I've impressed on him that you want more specific information than he's been able to give you so far.'

'Fine,' I said.

I turned back to the window. The girl must have seen the expression in my eyes because she said quickly, 'Something wrong?'

I nodded.

'Lots of things.'

The girl made a little pattern on the dull green carpet with the toe of her shoe.

'Like what?'

I came over close to her and stared down into those strange, violet eyes. She half-closed her eyelids as though she felt my gaze too penetrating.

'Like the reasons that made Mr Zangwill destroy all those death-notes he got, instead of calling the police. Why the people demanding the money should have chosen a place like the mausoleum, which was inside such strongly-guarded grounds.'

The girl's eyes were wide open now.

'You don't think anyone inside the house had something to do with it?'

'It's possible,' I said. 'Take a look at that.'

I stepped over to the window, the girl following.

'There couldn't be anything more public than that mausoleum.'

Laura Billington's face wore an expression of deep puzzlement.

'I don't quite understand, Mike. I get your point, though. If anyone tried to pick up the money he could be seen from here.'

'That's right,' I said. 'But you could turn it round another way.'

The girl flushed faintly.

'I'm listening.'

'Someone standing here could see when you or Mr Zangwill put the money in the mausoleum and could make sure, with a pair of the right field-glasses, that there was no-one in hiding there.'

I frowned down at the blanched whiteness of the mausoleum.

'The same situation would obtain after dark. Night-glasses would do the trick.'

The girl caught her breath in with a funny little noise. She shivered.

'That's horrible. You're surely not saying that Mrs Meakins or . . .'

I shook my head.

'I'm not specifying anyone, Laura. I'm just giving you a few of the thoughts that occurred to me.'

The secretary's face was dark and troubled now. She drew away from me a little, keeping her eyes on mine.

'You have some more points also, don't you?'

I nodded grimly.

'Dozens. This case is all questions and no answers. Doesn't it seem strange to you that you were attacked outside the grounds? What could you have possibly been carrying in the car that would have attracted an intruder? Unless you had money with you. An instalment on the demand in the note, shall we say?'

The girl had gone white. She clenched her small hands convulsively like she meant to strike me.

'Don't say that, Mike. I swear there was nothing like that. Mr Zangwill was determined not to pay.'

I gave her a long look.

'I believe you,' I said. 'But it still doesn't make sense. Let's take some more points.'

I lit a cigarette and put the spent matchstalk back in the box. I blew a whorl of smoke up toward the ceiling.

'You say Mr Zangwill has got the most elaborate electronic alarm equipment guarding the estate. He also has a very hard-looking guard and an even more effective Dobermann. Yet someone got in the grounds without any trouble at all.'

The girl's eyes were wide with surprise; she just stood silently as though afraid to break the stillness in here.

'Even more remarkably, that person got out again without any difficulty, without being apprehended by either the dog or the man.'

The girl shook her head somewhat defiantly, the soft brown hair a faint halo round her face in the light from the window.

'We've been through all that, Mike. You had the story from me, from Mr Zangwill and from Kempton.'

'That's true,' I said. 'But it still doesn't satisfy me. It all happened too easily.'

The girl's eyes were angry now.

'Maybe, Mike. But you forget that I was physically assaulted, shots were fired. People were in danger.'

'I'm not forgetting it,' I said.

Laura Billington's face was clearing now.

'You mean it might be someone who knows the estate well? A former employee, maybe?'

I nodded.

'Perhaps. I hadn't overlooked the point.'

The scarred face of the chauffeur Bassett in the picture in Mrs Meakins' sitting-room came back to me. The room must be almost directly underneath the one in which we were standing. I could imagine her still sitting there in the gloomy silence. Unless she was bustling around the kitchen preparing yet another of her ritual teas for some other member of the staff. The face of Bertram came back to me again; superimposed over the younger face in the photograph. As I'd seen him yesterday in that seedy bungalow, a few seconds before the place went up. He was one of the world's losers all right.

He'd taken on something too big. He wasn't cut out for blackmail. But it was crazy to suppose two groups of people were putting the bite on the old man; unless Bertram had broken away and decided to go into business for himself. Or whatever his real name was. I couldn't remember what the housekeeper had called him now. There was something else too, gnawing at the edges of my mind.

'There's only one real candidate,' Laura Billington said. 'Surely two years is too long to hold a grudge like that.'

I looked at her in silence for a second.

'Perhaps,' I said. 'But we're missing an important point here. What these people feel they've got on Zangwill. The character I saw yesterday mentioned photographs. If it doesn't mean anything to you it must mean something to the old man. If he doesn't come up with something in the next half-hour I'll have to ask him.'

The girl's lower lip suddenly trembled like she knew what I was talking about.

'I swear it means nothing to me, Mike. I don't see why it should mean anything to my employer.'

I nodded.

'Fair enough. If you've no objection we'll put it to the test.'

The Billington number firmed her chin.

'We've got to get at the truth,' she said softly.

'I'm glad we're agreed on something,' I said.

We were still standing close together at the window when the room door opened softly and old man Zangwill came in. He looked at us like a caricature of an owl beneath his thatch of white hair.

'My turn to find you out, Mr Faraday,' he said jovially.

2

He sat down at his desk and motioned us over like he was a teacher and we were a couple of high school pupils. I felt like one too as we sat down on a divan facing the desk. It was a good deal lower than the old man's seat, as he no doubt meant it to be and I remembered Hitler's set-up in the Chancellery in Berlin where the seating arrangements gave him a psychological advantage over the Heads of State and Ambassadors who came to see him there. But I guess I shouldn't press the analogy too far.

Zangwill folded his big hands on his blotter and looked at the pair of us solemnly, like he'd caught us out in something reprehensible. The haunted look had gone from his features.

'Miss Billington had a long talk with me yesterday, Mr Faraday,' he said. 'She put it to me rather forcibly that I had given you very little to go on in the matter of my commission.'

'That's the understatement of the year,' I said.

I leaned over and tapped half an inch of ash from the end of my cigarette into a square crystal tray on the low table in front of the divan.

'Point accepted,' Zangwill said calmly.

For a moment I caught a flash of the big

captain of industry he must have been the day before yesterday.

'I don't usually leave people who work for me in the dark like that. The truth is that I've been greatly tried in my past life. And the strain of the last few months has begun to tell on me.'

'Perhaps you'd feel better if you'd talk about it,' I said. 'Tell me what the contents of those notes really referred to.'

The old man's face went pale and he bit his lip, his dark eyes seeking the girl's.

'You're a shrewd man, Mr Faraday. But I really have little to add. Like I told you I tore them up, together with the envelopes as soon as they came. Surely the one you have is enough to be going on with.'

'My secretary's doing her best,' I said. 'But we won't get very far that way. Let's leave it for the moment. I've just been giving Miss Billington the benefit of my thoughts on the matter. She hasn't been very helpful either.'

The girl turned a startled face to me but I went on without stopping.

'I don't mean she's being obstructive. I think she's as much in the dark as I am.'

The old man's face was knotted with concentration.

'I'm not sure I follow.'

'I'm not surprised,' I said. 'Like I told Miss Billington none of this makes sense. The people who threatened you apparently didn't

122

say why they wanted your life. Or why you should give them money to spare it, for that matter. On top of that they asked for the money to be left inside a closely guarded estate, in a place which is easily overlooked from this room here and from many other rooms in the house I should imagine.'

Zangwill's face had gone paler and paler as I proceeded and his fingers had started trembling again like they'd done on my first visit. I didn't intend to let up now so I went on.

'Miss Billington was attacked outside the grounds. That doesn't make sense either. And the person who tried to break in easily eluded guard, dog and electronic devices. What does that look like?'

The old man clenched his jaw and made an effort at firmness.

'An inside job, Mr Faraday.'

I looked at him approvingly.

'Excellent,' I said. 'Now we're getting somewhere. The question is, why should it be an inside job?'

I'd made up my mind now and I plunged on while they were both off balance.

'I met a man yesterday,' I said. 'That was the reason I couldn't come out here. He tried to get me to shake you down for half a million too. He said he'd got some photographs that you'd pay that sort of cash to have suppressed.'

There was an extraordinary expression on Zangwill's face now; if I hadn't thought the idea even crazier, I'd have said he was relieved. He half-rose from his chair, putting the big palms of his hands flat on the tooled leather surface of the desk.

'This is astonishing, Mr Faraday. It is incredible. I know nothing of such material.'

'You're certain of that,' I said.

A strange glance passed between Laura Billington and her employer. She half-rose too.

'If there's something you'd rather talk about in private with Mr Faraday, I can withdraw,' she said in a low voice.

The old man stared at her as though he couldn't believe his ears. Little patches of red were standing out on his cheeks.

'If you mean what I think you mean, Laura,' he said evenly, 'I prefer to forget what you just said. I can assure both of you that there is nothing in my past in the photographic field that would cause any of us within this room a moment's concern.'

The girl looked embarrassed. She sat down again rather too quickly.

'I'm sorry, Mr Zangwill. I'm not implying anything. It was just that I didn't know what Mr Faraday was inferring. But I can still leave if you'd rather.'

Zangwill shook his head stubbornly.

'I want to know what Mr Faraday means,' he said grimly. 'Who was this man, Mr Faraday? Bring him here and I'll confront him.'

I shook my head.

'I can't do that, Mr Zangwill. He's dead now. He died rather violently. And I'm lucky to be here myself.'

There was shock on both their faces. The old man put his hands together in front of him and knotted his fingers convulsively.

'I seem to have gotten you into something rather deadly, Mr Faraday,' he said slowly. 'If you want to withdraw . . .'

I shook my head.

'It's my business,' I said. 'But I just like to know what I'm getting into. I'd appreciate absolute frankness from your side of the table.'

The old man's fingers had stopped trembling. He looked at me almost sadly.

'I can say quite sincerely that I know nothing of the man you mention. I certainly know nothing of any photographs that might embarrass me, financially or otherwise. And what you say about this violence or the events at this house are equally obscure.'

He was so patently sincere in what he was saying that I believed him at once. I looked from him to the girl. There was no sound in the room except for the faint pattering of rain at the windows and the low crackle of the fire.

'That's settled then, Mr Zangwill,' I said. 'We won't mention it again. But it still leaves me with a hundred loose ends.'

The old man's eyes were calm as he stared at me from under his shock of white hair.

125

'You do know the name of the man who died yesterday?' he said.

I nodded.

'It's already been in the papers. But it's not his real name. I can't see any point in going into it all now until I get the facts straight. It's only one of a hundred questions I want answering. If I could find these photographs it would be different.'

I paused but the bleak eyes gave me no encouragement. Old man Zangwill had put on the iron mask again.

'It's my guess he's left the stuff in a locker in a bus-station or an airport somewhere. You sure there's nothing that could compromise you? In the business or political field perhaps?'

The old man was grinning now.

'I met Hitler once,' he said. 'In the early thirties. It was in all the papers. He was trying to buy manganese and copper for his armaments industries. It was a bad scene, you might say. But I didn't sell him any. That's on public record too.'

I smiled back at him.

'I don't think that's what we're talking about,' I said. 'I'd like to ask about your close family history.'

Again the guarded look between employer and employee. Old man Zangwill's hair was like dusty dead weed in the firelight.

'Fire away,' he said.

CHAPTER TWELVE

1

I lit another cigarette from the butt of my old one and put the first in the tray.

'Mrs Meakins mentioned you had a nephew who's an architect,' I said.

The old man nodded. His eyes had softened now.

'My sister-in-law Ann's boy,' he said. 'I was very fond of her. She was a tremendous help in my early career. Unfortunately, my wife's death changed everything.'

He hesitated and his voice trembled.

'She was staying here at the time of the ...'

'The accident,' Laura Billington said softly.

He gave her a grateful glance.

'To my astonishment she afforded me none of the support to which I felt I was entitled in the middle of the tragedy. In fact, a short while after the funeral, she packed her bags and left.'

He looked at me sombrely.

'Not to put too fine a point on it, we lived estranged for more than forty years.'

I watched my smoke rising in spirals toward the ceiling.

'You mean she's dead, then?' I said. 'I had hoped I might get her impressions of this business.'

The old man shook his head.

'She died almost a year ago. My nephew is friendly enough. I've seen him on and off over the years. Always here. I was never invited to them and Ann never again set foot on the estate, even to attend the services we hold annually on the anniversary of her sister's death.'

I felt the girl's eyes on my face but I didn't break the silence. The old man went on like we weren't here.

'I asked Joshua a few times why his mother never came. In a tactful manner, of course. He was just as puzzled and pained in his own way as I was.'

'So you never found out?' I said.

Zangwill shook his head.

'It's been a mystery from that day to this. We shall never know now. Women were always a closed book to me, Mr Faraday. Apart from my wife. I was blessed in her.'

There was such naked pain in his voice I felt obliged to look away. The girl slid her hand along the divan and put it on mine. It was small and chill against the warmth of my flesh.

'You're a young man, Mr Faraday,' Zangwill said. 'Contrary to general belief, there's no wisdom or peace in age.'

'That's what Eliot says,' I told him. *'What was to be the value . . . the long hoped for calm, the wisdom of age.'*

The trembling of the old man's fingers had

stopped. His eyes were fixed upon me in a profound look.

'You are most unexpected for a private detective, Mr Faraday,' he said.

'It's not an exact quote,' I said. '*The Quartets*, I think.'

Zangwill nodded and there was another heavy silence.

'Where were we, Mr Faraday?' he said absently.

'Getting the answers to a few questions,' I said. 'This is much more satisfactory than a couple of days ago.'

'Maybe,' the old man said gravely. 'But unfortunately, I find it a great deal more painful.'

'Perhaps we could leave it for now,' the girl said quickly. 'Mrs Meakins will have tea in a few minutes.'

'I haven't quite finished,' I said gently. 'I'd like to speak to your nephew. That is, if you have no objections.'

Zangwill folded his hands peacefully together on the blotter. He looked completely self-possessed now.

'None at all, Mr Faraday,' he said softly. 'Though what he will be able to tell you is anybody's guess. You'll find him in the directory. He's in practice here in L.A.'

He looked at me mildly.

'But I'd appreciate it if you said nothing to him of the trouble I'm in. He's a great worrier.'

I smiled at the old man and the girl.

'I'll be discreet,' I said.

2

It was around five o'clock when I left. The girl
came with me to the front door. The old man
had excused himself and had gone to his room.

'You've got the address all right?' she said.

'Joshua Cameron?' I said. 'Sure. I have it
here.'

I tapped my wallet.

'I feel we're getting somewhere at last,
Mike,' Laura Billington said.

I smiled faintly.

'Glad you think so,' I said. 'Not from where
I'm sitting.'

She shrugged.

'Nevertheless, you've made some progress.
Though I don't know why you were so
mysterious about that man who was killed.'

'There is a reason,' I said. 'Never tip your
hand too soon. Someone concerned with this
business knows I've traced him out. But there's
no point in letting everyone know for the
moment.'

The girl's face was grave again. We were
standing in the wide immensity of the hall and
she had her head on one side like she was
listening for a distant footfall in the mansion.

'You're staking yourself out, then,' she said.

'Whoever killed the man you were interviewing knows you're on to something. He may go for you next.'

'It's a possibility,' I said. 'Does it worry you, Laura?'

The girl's face was turned up to mine. She moved closer and I felt the supple strength of her shoulders beneath my fingers. The kiss was a long and deep one and when I came back to the floor again she pushed me gently away. Her violet eyes were liquid and appealing now.

'It does worry me, Mike,' she said softly. 'I wouldn't want anything to happen to you.'

'Neither would I,' I said. 'I'll bear it in mind.'

She smiled again and stepped back from me.

'What are you going to do now?'

'See the nephew,' I said. 'Tomorrow. He may remember something relevant.'

'How do you know the man who was killed didn't write the blackmail notes?' Laura Billington said.

'I don't,' I told her. 'But it stands to reason things won't finish here. The people who took him out have an interest in the matter. I figure he was trying to muscle in on something too big for him.'

The girl turned her face up to me again.

'There are things you haven't told us,' she said. 'You've got some ideas of your own about this.'

I nodded.

'A lot of possibilities are rattling around inside my mind. But I'm going to leave them for the time being. It's safer for everyone that way.'

The girl inclined her head. There was a satisfied look on her face now.

'You mean it's safer for me and Mr Zangwill, don't you?'

'It sure as hell is that,' I said.

The girl opened the door and the dimness and the rain and the damp, decaying smell the wind brought with it added a melancholy dimension to the scene. Laura Billington wrinkled up her nose in distaste.

'Fancy having to work all these problems out. And under these conditions too! I wouldn't know where to begin.'

I smiled.

'It's my job,' I told her. 'But you have a point. Is there anything you haven't mentioned?'

The girl shook her head.

'Nothing important that I can think of. I still don't understand about the photographs. I'm sure Mr Zangwill was telling the truth about them.'

I scuffed at the tiled floor with my shoe. It made a brittle, melancholy noise in the silence of the great hall. Mrs Meakins was nowhere in evidence now. I pictured her still amid the dimness and the silence of her sitting-room.

She'd glided out at tea-time and I'd had no further opportunity of speaking with her.

'So am I,' I said.

'Funny about the photographs,' the girl said. 'Mrs Cameron was a great photographer.'

I looked at her blankly.

'I don't understand.'

'Mrs Zangwill's sister. She was always taking pictures around the estate, according to him. Of course, I didn't know her. But she was a brilliant photographer in her way. She took a number of studies of Mr Zangwill and his wife. And nature shots on the estate, of course. We still have them hanging about the house.'

3

I stared at her a second longer. A faint echo was stirring at the back of my brain.

'I'd like to see one,' I said. 'It may be nothing but it's as well to check.'

The girl looked at me in puzzlement.

'We've got some in the office here.'

She slammed the front door and led the way back with quick, staccato steps. Inside the study she hurried up the gallery. I followed on behind. She put on a light switch somewhere between the bookstacks and the room was flooded with light.

'These are two of Mr Zangwill's favourites.'

I soon saw what she meant. They were

large, sepia studies, obviously taken in the thirties, and elaborately mounted and framed in silver. One was a shot of stormy skies over the lake. The mausoleum wasn't there, obviously, but she'd exposed and framed the shot so that the place looked like something out of a fantasy painting by Dulac or Arthur Rackham.

I don't know a lot about such things but the more I looked at the picture the more I realized Mrs Cameron had the makings of a great camera artist.

The other was more conventional, but just as striking in its way. It was taken at the lake-edge and depicted Zangwill and his wife. He stood holding the bridle of a high-spirited-looking horse. Astride the animal was a tall, blonde woman; she was one of the most beautiful things I'd ever seen. I couldn't take my eyes off her. The girl caught the look in my eye.

'Lovely, wasn't she?'

I nodded.

'That isn't the word. I can see why Zangwill had a life-long passion for her.'

I crossed the gallery to a small circular window and stared down at the white mausoleum by the lake. Then I re-joined the girl by the pictures again and frowned at them. I saw they were signed in pencil; A.C. Again the girl interpreted my glance.

'Ann Cameron,' she said. 'Good, wasn't

she?'

'One of the best,' I said.

I turned back to the study of Zangwill and his wife.

'That was the horse?'

'On which she had the accident?'

Laura Billington inclined her head.

'He had the beast destroyed, as I think I told you.'

She turned away to face the small window at the end of the gallery.

'Such pictures as these were painful to him after. But he couldn't bear to lock them away. So, he had them banished to places like this. He doesn't use the study much these days.'

There was a long, heavy silence between us. To break it I moved back toward the window.

'Would you like to see some more examples of Ann Cameron's work?' the girl asked at last.

I shook my head.

'No point. Not today, at any rate. What sort of architecture does the nephew do?'

'Private houses, mostly,' the girl said. 'He's in a pretty big way, I understand.'

'It's hard not to make money as an architect in California if you're any good,' I said.

I was talking for effect now. Something was holding me up on the gallery here but I wasn't quite sure what it was. And it hadn't merely to do with the fact that I was reluctant to go out into the bleak atmosphere and the hammering rain of outdoors again. I moved forward and took up my former position in front of the circular window. It was so high up here that even the tops of the trees in the park were far below. It was almost like flying low in a helicopter except that the scene was stationary.

I stared at the blanched whiteness of the mausoleum again like it held the key to all my problems. As I did so, something black flickered past it. I stared, focusing my eyes. It was a tall, dark figure. I knew it wasn't the boy I'd seen guarding the gate this afternoon.

'How many people you got on sentry-go out here today?' I said.

The girl was at my side now.

'Just the man at the gate, Mike.'

The figure had gone into the mausoleum now.

'No-one else has authority to be in the grounds?' I said.

Something of my urgency had communicated itself to Laura Billington.

'Not that I know of. What's the matter?'

'Someone's down there now,' I said. 'Someone who shouldn't be. He's inside the mausoleum. I'm going to take a look.'

The girl's face had fear on it as she shrank back, her eyes fixed through the darkness of the wavering tree-tops.

'Maybe it's him? The man at the gate.'

I shook my head.

'Nothing like him. Get on the phone to the lodge and warn the man there. But tell him to be careful and that I'm around. We don't want any accidents.'

There was a faint smile on the girl's face now as she went clattering down the gallery steps. I was a couple of treads behind her.

'Take care, Mike.'

I tapped my breast-pocket, felt the bulk of the Smith-Wesson.

'I can handle it. Better tell your man I'm armed. The two of us should be able to take care of it.'

Laura Billington nodded. She was already at the desk, reaching for the phone as I got to the door. I grabbed my raincoat from the peg in the vestibule and buttoned it. I got the Smith-Wesson and put it in my right-hand pocket, where I could get at it in a hurry.

The wind and the rain met me with more than physical force; it was almost like a psychic aura that battered at me. It wasn't only the noise of water running and splashing off the big domed cupola of the porch; or the myriad drops hitting the foliage; or even the wind that was rocking the dark tops of the trees. It was something to do with the whole atmosphere of the estate and its history.

It had something of Zangwill's sadness and his wife's tragedy in it. The steel-grey waters of the lake were ruffled like a miniature sea as I pounded down the zig-zag concrete path between the trees that led to the shimmering white mirage of the mausoleum in the far distance.

CHAPTER THIRTEEN

1

I was soaked through before I'd gone a hundred yards. The rain had a dense, penetrating quality; it drifted like smoke or mist in the tree-tops, agitated by the wind, and when it came to earth it was like a miniature cloudburst which enveloped one completely. I followed the looping path; it might take me fractionally longer. But the lawns and the walks through the undergrowth would be a quagmire and I'd make heavier progress.

I hadn't been able to keep my eye on the mausoleum but I felt fairly sure the person I'd seen was still in there, though he might have slipped away during the time the building was hidden from sight between intervening belts of trees. But I was relying on the heaviness of the downpour to muffle the noise of my progress on the heavy paving slabs.

My heart was pounding and once my foot skidded on some lichen on one of the flag-stones so that I almost did a spectacular somersault at a turn of the path. I was out on the lakeside now and the wind was shouting, blowing the rain into my eyes and chilling my face and body. I wondered whether the young guy had left the lodge yet.

I hoped he wouldn't be too trigger-happy. Like I told the girl it could be tricky out here this afternoon and I didn't want any slip-ups. Either way that is. I didn't want to get dead myself but equally I didn't want to have to explain to the L.A. Police why I'd shot a security guard on the Zangwill estate and let an intruder go. It wouldn't look good when my licence came up for renewal.

I was out in the open, unfortunately, as I rounded the end of the lake and anyone in the mausoleum must have seen me if he'd been facing this way. I put my elbows down and sprinted, keeping to the grass to minimize the sound, though I had to get back on the path almost immediately to avoid slipping. It was inevitable that some of the noise I was making should reach whoever was prowling around inside the white marble building, but I had to risk that.

Still there was no sign of life from that direction. Then I got behind a clump of trees again and when I re-emerged the mausoleum was only about a hundred yards away. I slackened my pace and went wide on the grass, making a circle on the landward side, to come in in rear. The only entrance to the place was that facing the lake and I would have an advantage when the intruder came out again.

My mind was drifting a little. It must have

been the exertion of running and the rain which was streaming down my face, but I had a sudden crazy notion that the man inside had come to see if the money had been left there like the note specified. So far as I knew no arrangements had been made with Zangwill; unless he'd been holding out on me regarding the notes. That was a possibility.

Of course, if things got worse and I ran out of leads we could always make up a dummy package and leave it as bait; but we were a long way from that stage.

That also left out of account how the intruder had gotten into the grounds without triggering the alarm and why he would come in daylight instead of after dark when the going would have been much easier from his point of view. I slackened speed and swung round; I was only about fifteen feet from the rear of the building and I eased on over the soggy turf, my heart pounding heavily, my fingers feeling the cool of the Smith-Wesson butt in my right-hand raincoat pocket. There was no sign of anything or anyone near the building.

There was also no sign of the young guard Laura Billington was supposed to have phoned; I found all sorts of dark thoughts chasing themselves around inside my skull and thrust them to the back of what was left of my mind. I felt the stonework wet and sticky against my left hand and I inched round the semi-circular wall to the right, listening

140

carefully. All I could hear though was the steady hiss of the rain and the splattering noise it made when it reached the grass.

Rain was running into my eyes and trickling down my collar. Apart from actually being in the lake I couldn't have been much wetter. I was about halfway round the building now, midway between the rear wall and the front right-hand entrance gate. If you were looking towards the lake, of course; from the lake it would be the left-hand gate. I don't know why I bothered with all these details. I guess I was just talking to myself.

I've found that there's nothing so demoralizing as being cold and wet on a case. Today was proving my point without much effort. It wouldn't have surprised me if the chambers of the Smith-Wesson had been filled with water too; it was that sort of afternoon. I stopped for a few seconds, straining my ears to make out any sound from the mausoleum.

There was nothing, like I figured. I started moving forward again. The rain was coming down in solid sheets, swathing the outlines of even the stonework just in front of my eyes. It was the worst kind of day and the worst kind of visibility. I was cursing my luck but nevertheless it was those two factors which saved my life.

The water of the lake to my right-hand front suddenly erupted into a fountain. At the same time something struck the stonework about two feet from my head, sending splinters of dust and grit into my face.

I hit the grass instinctively and the third slug, intended for my throat, struck the wall instead, a little higher up. The sour taste of fear was in me but the adrenalin pumping through my veins sent me rolling and slithering across the turf. I got inside the front entrance of the mausoleum in about three seconds flat as the fourth shot cracked out but that made a hole in the lake-water too.

I had the Smith-Wesson up and my heart was pumping unsteadily. It was some marksman out there. I guessed then he'd slipped out the mausoleum while I was passing the last clump of trees, and gone to ground in a thicket about fifty yards away. I shouldn't have been here now but for the rain and the difficult sighting conditions. I felt sweat trickle down my forehead among the cold beads of rainwater.

It was as near a thing as I'd ever experienced and I felt angry with myself as the reaction came over me; I strained my eyes round the edge of the stone entrance wall toward the thick clumps of bushes away to the right, my fingers trembling slightly on the Smith-Wesson butt.

I couldn't see anything. It was useless without a target and I lowered the weapon. Slight as the motion was it alerted someone out there in the misty rain. I didn't hear the slap of the shot, probably because the wind was gusting and blowing the sound in the other direction, but something spanged viciously off the metal gate only a yard from where I was kneeling, and went whining out over the lake.

I got back inside the entrance to the mausoleum, doing some fast thinking. Staying here was one way of committing suicide quickly. Yet to try to get out along the front was to invite an even quicker death. The first-class marksman securely hidden in the darkness of the trees had got me pegged. If the gateman didn't turn up soon it was only a question of time before the hitman would shift round so that he could aim directly into the mausoleum through the opening in front.

I had an idea myself then. My eyes were adjusted to the lowered intensity of the light in here and I glanced round the interior. I hadn't even bothered when I'd come in because it was obvious the man who'd come in here was now shooting from outside; even more conclusive proof was the set of wet shoe-marks which circled the sarcophagus and then went on out down the front steps and disappeared to the left. Everything pointed to an inside job this afternoon; it was all of a piece with everything else that had happened.

I was left too with an ugly image of Laura Billington making like busy at the telephone. She hadn't made the call by the time I'd left the office and maybe she'd never made it. I thrust that picture to the back of my mind too. I had enough problems this afternoon. What I was looking at without seeing it was the large, circular window set high up in the wall on my side of the burial chamber.

It overlooked the grove of trees among which my man was crouched and if I could get up there I would have a big advantage. Firstly, it was dark inside the dome and I could see out without being seen. Secondly, my man would have no reason to know I'd shifted position and he'd still be looking for me around the front steps.

Thirdly, and most importantly, I'd be in a good position to see if he left the shelter of the trees and went across the grass. Fourthly, I'd be up out of sight in the dome if he suddenly decided to rush my shelter.

He didn't know I was armed, which was perhaps my biggest advantage for the moment. Fifthly, and another decisive point, was the fact that he'd already pumped five shots. It depended whether he had a five or six chamber revolver but he'd be re-loading about now which seemed the clinching factor in my changing position. All this had passed through my mind in fractions of seconds and I got up and went across the floor of the mausoleum at a run.

I took off in great style and got my hands over the rim of the stonework beneath the window; my shoes scrabbled against the wall and then I hoisted myself up; I was on the sill which was over a foot wide, making a comfortable seat. The window was partly stained glass too and I could get behind the red-robed figure of a saint which would effectively screen me from anyone looking toward the building from outside.

I stared through a sheet of clear glass. I had a fine view of the lake surround, the path leading along it and the lawn with the group of trees and shrubs in the centre and from which my opponent had been firing. I got my Smith-Wesson out my pocket and laid it down on the ledge close to my hand. I felt a draught now and found one of the leaded lights had worked loose at the far right-hand corner of the circular window.

It left an aperture about four inches square which would be great to shoot through if I had to. I strained my eyes through the dim light and the falling rain and raked across the heavy green of the group of trees. It was almost impossible to make out any detail because of the deep shadow. The man who'd got into the grounds had chosen his terrain well. Which proved that he knew something about it.

I wondered, for the second or third time since I'd come out, whether I'd been deliberately decoyed from the house; which would imply a degree of collusion between two or more people. Once again Laura Billington's image flickered across my mind and for the third or fourth time I brushed it away. The whole thing was too convenient; my spotting the man down at the lake could have been coincidence, of course, but he could have set himself out as bait.

The man in the bushes might even be a second gunsel, hired to cover the escape of the first. That hadn't slipped my attention but the prospect was a bit forbidding and it wasn't one I was anxious to entertain. I could just about manage one, under these conditions; but two would be two too many.

I shifted my position slightly, picking up the Smith-Wesson and advancing it cautiously toward the small hole in the bottom of the window. Again I raked my gaze across the dark belt of foliage. I figured the marksman would be reasonably dry and warm, beneath the bottom branches of one of the thicker trees, resting at the foot of the trunk and with a fairly clear view from the dark shadow, across the close-cropped turf to the side and front of the mausoleum.

That's why he was so well-placed. The building was at an oblique angle from where he was stationed so that he would be able to command the front flight of steps along which I'd have to run to escape. There was no way I could get out alive unless he got tired and went away or I waited until after dark. Neither alternative was a very alluring prospect.

In the event the problem was solved for me. I'd sat there for ten minutes, with the tension slowly ebbing away from the atmosphere. It was then that I heard the high whine of gears and the sound of a throbbing motor as a vehicle came bouncing and jolting across the grass.

CHAPTER FOURTEEN

1

I jumped down from the ledge and ran to the front of the mausoleum. A station wagon was lurching slowly along the lake-edge, keeping to the path where possible but going across the grass where it made the shortest route. The two arcs made by the windscreen wipers looked like staring eyes in the gloom. I looked round the entrance pillar, to the right, thought I saw a dark shadow flicker away between the trees.

The station wagon was up near the building now, grinding to a halt. The near-side door opened hesitantly and the head of the blond boy thrust out.

'That you, Mr Faraday? I thought I heard shooting.'

'For Christ's sake!' I said. 'You took your time.'

I ducked out the mausoleum, running down the steps in the rain and almost took a header into the passenger seat. The blond boy's face expressed alarm and surprise as he saw the Smith-Wesson but his manner was firm enough.

'You heard shooting all right,' I said. 'I was pinned down. You better get after him if Mr Zangwill doesn't mind his grass being torn up.'

The blond boy was better on action than words. He slammed in the gear and took the wagon off the lake path and up on to the grass, skidding and slithering toward the clump of trees. His main beams stabbed the gloom. Like I figured, there was nothing there now.

'He'll be making for the edge of the grounds,' I said. 'You know the lay-out.'

The blond boy nodded, his eyes bright.

'Pretty well, Mr Faraday. Mr Zangwill won't mind his grass being torn up under the circumstances. Normally I'd have come on foot but it seemed urgent and it's no sense getting drowned under these conditions.'

He had a point there. I concentrated on looking through the windscreen arc as we slowly jolted round the screen of trees; I had the Smith-Wesson up but nothing showed.

'You took your time,' I said again.

The boy's eyes glinted as he glanced at me.

'I'm sorry about that, Mr Faraday. I was out front on patrol and I didn't get Miss Billington's phone message until just a couple of minutes ago. She should have used the walkie-talkie.'

I stared at him in silence, my mind absorbing the information.

'She wasted fifteen minutes like that,' the blond boy said.

He looked worriedly through the wiper-arc as he steered us closer to a thick wall of foliage which was slowly coming up the sky-line.

'Perhaps she didn't think of it,' I said.

The boy shrugged, changing gear again as the tyres skidded on the wet grass.

'Maybe,' he said simply.

His heavy silence implied criticism. It gave me something to think about too.

'Can you use that rifle?' I said.

I was looking at the powerful job he had in a leather bucket fixed inside the driving door.

The boy's eyes gleamed again.

'Try me, Mr Faraday.'

'You'll get your chance,' I said.

He shot me a swift glance.

'What happened? Miss Billington said you spotted an intruder down by the lake? Sounded screwy to me.'

'I nearly got jumped,' I said. 'He pumped

five shells at me. If it hadn't been for the rain and the bad visibility I'd have been lying back there now. He had me pinned down in the mausoleum until you came along. He was working from that big clump of trees in the middle of the lawn.'

The blond boy's lips drew together in a thin line.

'Good shot, you say?'

'The best,' I said.

The boy broke into a lazy grin.

'I'm pretty good myself with the rifle. Maybe we'll try him out.'

He turned the wheel and the station wagon groaned and lurched its way down a narrow path between the boles of great trees. It was dark in this forest ride and the headlamp beams bored two deep tunnels of yellow incandescence so that it seemed like we were travelling along some underground passage.

He'll be making for the wall,' the blond boy said. 'The trees overhang along here. It's a weak spot which the old man was always going to have fixed. But I can't understand how the electronics failed to pick him up.'

'We'll go into that later,' I said.

That was when the windscreen starred, there was a harsh cracking noise and the whole world began to cartwheel.

2

I got up to find the station wagon at an insane angle. I'd been thrown clear and was lying on a bank that seemed to be mainly composed of soft grass and pine needles. I still had the Smith-Wesson in my hand so I loosed off a shot into the air, more for the sake of morale than anything else. I was feeling pretty shaken, come to that.

The blond boy appeared at my elbow. He was none the worse for wear except that he was smothered in mud from head to foot. He was swearing and there was a wild look in his eyes.

'The cunning bastard,' he said emotionlessly. 'He's taken on the wrong people.'

He sighted along the barrel and got off a quick shot. There was a crisp, clean detonation and splinters jumped off the bark of a tree about two hundred yards away along the aisle. The gun had a pump action and he got two more shots off before I spotted something zigzagging away, bent low, far off along the ride.

The blond boy grunted with satisfaction. He must have had eyes like a hawk. I hadn't seen a thing until then. He turned to me with a lazy motion.

'You'd best leave this to me, Mr Faraday.

That peasshooter won't be much use under these conditions.'

'You may be right. Make the play. I'll stay right beside you.'

'He won't be hanging around,' the boy said. 'Just try and keep up.'

He went off like a hare, jumping easily over tree-boles and fallen branches. I pounded after him, still holding the Smith-Wesson, knowing how useless it was, like the boy had said. But it was good for morale. And I knew the man who'd tried to trigger me would be fighting for his own life now. Because his weapon was useless against a powerful rifle used by a trained marksman like this boy, whose eyes were even better than mine.

There likely wouldn't be much danger now but I wanted to be around to act as back-up in case the boy got into trouble. Not that it seemed likely at this stage. But one never knew. He was about fifteen feet ahead of me now, jumping fallen tree-trunks like an Olympic athlete, the rifle held clear in his right hand.

He swerved suddenly and went into bushes at the side of the ride. He turned as I came up.

'We'd best keep under cover now, Mr Faraday. He'll make for the wall and we'll maybe cut him off.'

'Just as you say,' I said. 'I don't know these grounds at all.'

We had both stopped now and I fancied I

could hear a faint crashing noise a long way ahead. The boy had heard it too. His face expressed satisfaction.

'He's on the run, Mr Faraday.'

'You all right?' I said.

He nodded.

'Just a shaking-up. I was thrown clear. I was pretty mad. That was why I wasn't shooting too good.'

'If this is one of your off days I wouldn't want to be around when you're shooting good,' I said. 'Leastways, not if I was at the other end of the barrel.'

He grinned, showing sharp white teeth. We were pounding on and I was beginning to feel the start of a stitch in my side. We were getting up toward the end of the ride now and the guard, who was in front, swerved suddenly to the right, gesturing to me at the same time. He was going at a suicidal pace, running blind through low undergrowth, clearing half-seen fallen logs instinctively.

I followed at a slower speed, not knowing the ground so well. I lost sight of him for a few seconds and then caught up. We were running alongside a high wall of red brick, with buttresses here and there. There was a tarmac path round the perimeter, hemmed in by heavy banks of rhododendron and greenery. It was an oppressive place and there was a cloying stench of rotting vegetation that even the freshness of the rain couldn't mask.

The blond boy stopped suddenly, gesturing me down. The foliage drew in across the path here, masking the way ahead. The boy pointed to the broken stem of a fern which lay across the path. It was just in the act of springing back into position. The tall boy put his mouth up against my ear.

'He's only just ahead,' he whispered. 'Tiring. We don't want to run up against him unawares.'

'You can say that again,' I said.

The guard stepped aside from the path now, motioning me to follow. He picked his way delicately, the slight noise his movements made masked by the falling rain. I followed as carefully as I could. It was only now I was realizing how tired and wet and beat-up I was. I guess the shoot-out and the crash just after had shaken me up worse than I thought. I felt my fingers trembling slightly again on the butt of the Smith-Wesson.

I put the safety on while I thought about it. The blond boy was capable of shooting the ear off a squirrel at five hundred yards and the Smith-Wesson wouldn't be much use in here, except at very close range. And I didn't aim to blow a hole clear through my thigh at this stage of my career. Such as it was. I grinned wryly to myself, following the lean guard closely. Despite the difficult conditions he was making good time and I tried to put my feet exactly where he'd trodden.

He stopped once for a few seconds, his head cocked on one side, his hand up enjoining caution. I froze where I was. The only sound I could hear was the patter of the rain and the pumping of my heart. Then the blond boy turned, his eyes shining.

'He's waiting for us at the turn of the path,' he said confidently. 'The cunning devil. We'll curve round to take him in rear.'

For the next five minutes we worked in a wide arc; it was deadly going among the soaking bushes and I wondered for the hundredth time why I hadn't taken up another profession that I could have followed indoors, preferably at a comfortable desk. The guard called a halt again when we'd worked around a long way. He shook his head.

'He knows this area as well as I do,' he said. 'He's out-guessing us all the time. He's moved on.'

He got back on the path, not bothering about noise any more. I had so much confidence in him that I followed without hesitation. We hurried along the tarmac in the dim light, keeping a keen eye for the slightest movement in the bushes. We came out into a biggish glade in which the trees drew back from the wall. Right at the end was a massive Spanish oak whose branches reached out across the path. The blond boy shook his head disappointedly.

'Too late, Mr Faraday. He's gone over.'

Even as he spoke a car gunned up somewhere on the road beyond the wall. We couldn't see anything because it was about twelve feet high. We stood there getting nice and wet in the steady downpour and listened to it whisper away down the mountain road.

'That's it, Mr Faraday,' the guard said.

We were standing like that when there was a sudden crackling noise in the bushes at our rear. The blond boy's rifle had swivelled like the gun-turret of a battleship as I spun on my heel.

CHAPTER FIFTEEN

1

I had the rifle barrel in my hand, pushed it upward as the guard swore.

'Take it easy,' I said. 'It's Miss Billington.'

There was a flash of white raincoat and the girl's frightened face was looking out at us. Her brown hair was dishevelled and almost black it was so soaked with rain. The blond boy grinned at me wryly and put the rifle barrel toward the ground.

'Thanks, Mr Faraday. I guess my nerves are a little on edge.'

He turned to face the girl as she came up, looking very small and vulnerable.

156

'You should be more careful, Miss. We don't want an accident.'

The girl looked from the boy's face to mine and shivered.

'This is a dreadful business. You didn't see who it was?'

I shook my head.

'He was too quick for us. But he knows the ground well. There may be something in that.'

The girl came close to me, put visibly shaking fingers on my arm.

'I couldn't stay in the house. I had to come down when I heard the shots.'

'I'd rather you'd stayed up there,' I said. 'But your courage does you credit. You haven't told the old man about this?'

'Of course not. Especially after what you said, Mr Faraday.'

She shook her head, small drops of water from her hair describing a glittering arc. The blond boy stood impassively, his face a mask of running rivulets. He reminded me of one of those classical fountains one finds in places like Rome. I guess I looked no better.

'We'd better get back to the house,' she said.

'Not until we find exactly how he got in,' I said.

The blond guard nodded, like he approved. He led the way down the path to where one of the huge branches of the oak came quite close to the top of the wall.

'We always meant to cut this back, Mr

Faraday. It's one of the weak places.'

I shook my head.

'Nevertheless, he didn't come that way. It's my guess he used a rope ladder with a grapnel.'

I pointed out the moss and lichen on the wall. In parts there were deep grooves dug in it, up and down the brick surface.

'That's where the toes of his boots scraped the moss away coming and going,' I said.

'You're right, Mr Faraday,' the young man said grudgingly.

He looked from me to the girl like he was waiting for some instructions.

'How would he get over?' the girl asked.

'Simply climb up from the outside, straddle the wall and then let the ladder down,' I said.

I looked sharply at the guard.

'You said something about the electronics just now.'

The boy seemed puzzled.

'That's what I can't understand. Without giving away the estate secrets, as soon as anyone got over the wall the alarm should sound. That includes sirens and the whole works.'

'We heard nothing,' I said.

The guard nodded, his keen eyes staring upward. He gave a muffled exclamation. I noticed then a small steel box screwed to the wall, about a foot below the coping.

'Part of your alarm system?' I said.

'You may not be able to see it from here, Mr Faraday, but there's a very small wire half-buried in the brickwork. Someone's severed it with a pair of special pliers.'

I smiled wryly at the girl.

'That's it, then. Someone who knew the alarm system inside out.'

'I don't quite understand,' the girl said, her head held up to the falling rain like some Victorian story-book picture of an unfortunate heroine. I had it then. An old childhood memory of a book-illustration of Maggie Tulliver in *The Mill on the Floss*. Though I didn't tell her that.

'It makes things both a little easier and a little more difficult for me,' I told her. 'Like I said, an inside job.'

Her mouth turned down at the corners like I'd told a questionable joke in front of old man Zangwill. We had all three turned and walked back down the length of the wall; each occupied by secret thoughts, oblivious now of the pervasive presence of the rain.

'Sorry about the estate car, Miss Billington,' the guard said, almost irrelevantly. 'How am I going to explain it to Mr Zangwill?"

The girl looked like she was coming out of deep shock. She pressed close to, my side, her hand resting on my arm. I could feel her trembling right down to my own fingertips.

'Don't worry about that,' she said. 'We'll get it repaired discreetly. I'll explain it away all right in the quarterly accounts.'

The guard looked at her with a grateful expression.

'I wouldn't want this to get around,' he said apologetically. 'I got a good security record until now.'

'You did great,' I said. 'They don't come any better.' There was a faint flush on his cheeks.

'You really think so, Mr Faraday?'

'I should have been killed but for you,' I said.

He grinned.

'You wouldn't like to put that in writing?'

'I'll put it in the form of a bottle of bourbon,' I said.

The girl smiled too, quickening her pace.

'We'll all have a drink when we get in. Let's get back to the house.'

2

I tooled the Buick off the main-stem and up into the parking lot of the Bryce Building. It was still raining this morning but it was nowhere as persistent as yesterday and there were even a couple of breaks in the clouds which let a better quality light through. I found an empty slot in front of the thirty-storey block of chrome, marble and concrete and killed the motor. I finished off my cigarette and listened to the faint whisper of water on the roof of the

Buick.

I wasn't beating out my brains today; just idling over in low gear. I'd found my various theories were getting in the way of the basics in old man Zangwill's problems. Leastways they had been his problems; they were mine now and I didn't like it. Not one bit. I'd never had a case in which I went around in such crazy circles. I stubbed out my butt in the dashboard tray, got out the car, locked it and pounded over toward the front entrance steps.

The lobby was bright, antiseptic and looked like something out of a brochure for a Swedish abortion clinic. In 1938, of course. The Swedes were so far in advance that we still haven't caught up with them. Not in this building at any rate. I ignored the retired Russian major-general wearing one of Zhukov's cast-off uniforms and padded over toward the big teak board screwed to the right-hand wall of the lobby.

That was avant-garde too. The board wasn't perpendicular, of course. It wasn't the sort of place. It was cantilevered out at an angle and at the base of it the concourse dropped away to rocks, falling water and tropical plants among which exotic and very expensive-looking fish swam in an aimless and desultory fashion.

I looked from the fountain to the falling rain outside and sighed. The crazily inclined board bore the tenants' names and floor-

161

numbers on highly polished plaques in bronze lettering; I wondered what happened when they wanted to alter something. They'd have a lovely job getting ladders out over the artificial lake. I glanced at the fish again. They looked as bored as I felt right now.

It was probably the reaction after yesterday. I found Parrott, Gimpel and Cameron in the end. They were in a section reserved for architects and were on the seventh floor if the boards meant anything. I retraced my steps over to the far side of the concourse where a set of chromed steel elevator cages sat and waited for one to come down.

It wasn't long before a cage descended at express speed and two elderly men and a blonde girl got out with slightly dazed expressions. I figured they'd come from the thirtieth floor in short order and were still suffering from jet-lag. I got in cautiously and soon found what it meant. I had no sooner hit the button than the door closed in a metallic blur and I shot skyward. I was still waiting for my stomach to arrive when I was decanted into a corridor that was apparently walled in silver lamé snoods.

That was what it looked like anyway. I didn't stop to examine them or I might have thrown up in the corridor. I went on down, listening to whining noises from the air-conditioning and the faint pecking of electric typewriters beyond the doors. Like always,

Cameron's set-up was up the far end, about a half-mile hike and I was pretty bushed by the time I got there. There was a nice view of the smog and the falling rain though.

I went in through a polished teak door that said PARROTT, GIMPEL AND CAMERON. Architects and Design Consultants. ENTER. The reception area was only slightly smaller than the concourse down below, except that it had leather divans scattered about; low, metal tables that looked like they'd come out of an engineering foundry; lots of tropical foliage writhing out of metal trunking; and very expensive-looking photographs of nasty, functional houses, presumably designed by the partnership, hanging on the walls.

I figured the staff might be just as functional as the furniture but I was wrong. There wasn't a straight line or an angle on the blonde number who wheeled down the room toward me. She wore a soft brown corduroy suit that seemed moulded to every curve of her body and her little leather half-boots beat a rhythmic tattoo on the parquet flooring.

She was tall, but not too tall and her straight blonde hair, with just a curve at the end of it, was the only metallic thing about her; its burnished brilliance caught the light and turned to a coppery sheen as she walked. She wore an open-neck silk shirt whose creamy shade set off the bronzed pillars of her throat; and her smooth, broad brow, light blue eyes, strongly moulded jaw and cheek-bones, together with the full lips and fine teeth proclaimed Scandinavian ancestry.

She had the very faintest accent as she held out her hand formally.

'Good morning. I'm Ingeborg Svenson. Whom do you wish to see?'

My façade almost cracked but I managed to preserve it. Her fingers were cool and sensuous against my palm. Her nails had pale pink varnish on them and there was a very expensive-looking gold and diamond ring on the engagement finger of her disengaged hand.

My disappointment must have showed on my face, because she smiled, giving me another view of those flawless teeth.

'My name's Faraday,' I said. 'I'm here to see Mr Joshua Cameron if he's not too busy.'

She put her head on one side as though she were appraising me.

'I think he'd see you, Mr Faraday, providing your intentions are serious.'

I grinned.

'My intentions are serious, Miss Svenson.'

Her eyes held mine, little sparks of amusement dancing in them.

'Perhaps I haven't expressed myself very well, Mr Faraday. Are you a client?'

I shook my head.

'Not exactly. But my business is serious. I think he'll see me all right.'

The girl looked dubious but she said

nothing, just led me across the big reception area to a leather-topped desk in the far corner, in an angle formed by a bookcase and a group of tropical plants. She sat down behind the desk and put her elegant hands together on the blotter in front of her.

'What is your function, Miss Svenson?' I said.

She gave me another view of the excellent teeth.

'I'm a design consultant, Mr Faraday, and a junior partner in Mr Cameron's practice. The receptionist stepped out for an hour to visit the dentist. The three architects work separately; we put up a package. Mr Cameron designs the house, I design everything that goes into it.'

'Very nice,' I said. 'But I'd still like to see him.'

'I'd still like to know why,' the girl said.

'It's strictly private,' I told her.

There was a slight dent in the façade now. She gave a small intake of breath and narrowed her eyes. This was a girl who could be difficult if she was crossed.

'Mr Faraday, you must see . . .' she began.

'Let's stop horsing around,' I said. 'I have a commission from his uncle, Mr Zangwill. Just tell him that.'

The blonde number seemed to come unglued. She sort of shivered at the desk and folded at the middle like she was on hinges.

'The millionaire?'

'I didn't know people were still impressed by millionaires,' I said.

Miss Svenson smiled.

'I'm the sort of person who's always impressed by millionaires, Mr Faraday. Perhaps it's because they have so much money.'

'Could be,' I said. 'It seems to go with the job.' She smiled again and got up from the desk. 'If you've been retained by the family I think Mr Cameron will see you without further delay.'

'That's what I figured,' I told her.

CHAPTER SIXTEEN

1

Cameron, when I got to meet him was a tall, good-looking man with even teeth, a ready smile and lots of curly black hair which clung to his skull in a thick mass, giving him a Roman aspect. He got up from behind a desk an acre wide and came down the length of his office to meet me. His handclasp was firm and crushing. I figured him for something of a sportsman because there were a lot of silver cups and other junk of that sort sitting around on shelves and in a glass case in the back of his desk.

'Good to see you, Mr Faraday. Miss Svenson tells me you've come on behalf of my uncle.'

'That's right,' I said.

The girl stood at a corner of Cameron's desk and looked somewhat uncertainly from one to the other of us. Cameron interpreted her glance correctly.

'I have no secrets from Miss Svenson, Mr Faraday. I'd like her to hear what you have to say if it's about my uncle.'

'I have no objection,' I said. 'Though I wouldn't want things to go beyond this room.'

Cameron nodded gravely, his grey eyes looking at me searchingly. He went around to sit in a big padded chair behind his desk, waving me to another in front. The girl sat down in an easy chair in front of another case of silver trophies at the right-hand side of the room. Cameron put his immaculately manicured finger-nails together on his blotter and frowned at the big drawing-board that glowed under the draughtsman's lamps. That was evidently where all the work was done.

'May I ask in what capacity my uncle engaged you, Mr Faraday?'

I nodded.

'You may, Mr Cameron. I'm a private detective. If you want to see my credentials . . .'

Cameron held up his hand.

167

'By no means, Mr Faraday. I'll take your word for it. If Uncle Adrian hired you then that's good enough for me.'

He smiled thinly, glancing at the statuesque figure of the girl who lolled elegantly in the chair.

'You'd hardly come to see me with that story if my uncle hadn't engaged your services.'

I grinned, reaching for my pack of cigarettes.

'Hardly,' I said.

I offered the package around. Both shook their heads.

'Neither of us smoke,' Cameron volunteered. 'But we have no objection if you want to.'

'Thanks,' I said. 'It's been one of those cases so far.'

I lit up and Cameron shoved the upturned metal lid of a typewriter ribbon container across the desk to me. I put my spent match-stalk in it and turned back to the girl.

'I understand your uncle and your mother were very close at one time but they became estranged around the time of Mr Zangwill's wife's death. I wonder if you could tell me something about it.'

I was speaking to Cameron but I kept my eye on the Svenson number. She had a distasteful look on her face now, like this was something she and Cameron had discussed.

The architect shrugged, smiling faintly.

'It's all a long time ago, Mr Faraday. You

must realize I hadn't even been born when my aunt died. So, how could I help . . .'

'I realize that,' I said. 'I wondered whether your mother had ever discussed your uncle with you.'

A shadow passed across Cameron's face. He leaned back in the chair and swivelled it to and fro, his eyes on his hands.

'Naturally, my uncle was mentioned over the years,' he began. 'My mother wasn't very keen on my going out there but we never had rows over it. Might I ask where all this is leading? And what it has to do, with your present assignment?'

I nodded, feathering blue smoke out my nostrils.

'You may, Mr Cameron. And I'll answer you in a minute. Right now I'd like to ask what your mother's attitude to her brother-in-law was.'

Cameron looked baffled. He rocked about again for a moment or two.

'I gathered there'd been some quarrel between them many years earlier,' he said. 'My mother was a very close, reserved person. She was never very specific.'

'But you must have had some feelings about it,' I said.

Cameron nodded, looking across at the blonde girl with a tender expression.

'I had lots of feelings about it, Mr Faraday. I had a very happy childhood. And I liked my uncle. My mother never took me there when I was a child. But as soon as I was conscious of my family and I became older I started to cultivate him. He's a great man in his own way, don't you think?'

I looked at him for a long moment.

'I think you're right, Mr Cameron,' I said. 'I haven't delved very closely into his background but anyone who comes up in that industrial climate must be very tough, very determined and have a tremendous streak of ambition. It was a pity he let the tragedy of his wife's death blight his life.'

Cameron nodded, his eyes on his finger-tips again.

'All great men have their flaws,' he said softly. 'My uncle's Achilles' heel was his love for his wife. It rebounded on him with her death. He just couldn't take it or accept it.'

I glanced across at the girl but she kept quiet. The faint patter of rain at the windows and the hum of the air-conditioning were the only sounds in here. The rest of the practice seemed to be sunk in sleep and I hadn't seen any more staff since I'd arrived.

'That mausoleum in the grounds is pretty morbid, wouldn't you say?'

Cameron shrugged, his eyes still on his finger-tips.

'Perhaps, Mr Faraday. But who are we to judge?'

He looked at me frankly.

'Now perhaps we could know know the reason you're here?' he said gently.

<h2 style="text-align:center">2</h2>

I had their attention now. Even the girl was sitting up ramrod straight in the easy chair.

'Your uncle's life's been threatened,' I said. 'I'd like a rundown on any of the people who worked at the estate in the past who might be implicated.'

Cameron was making notes on a pad on the blotter in front of him now. The pencil in his lean, sensitive fingers raced across the paper.

'I'm not sure I understand this, Mr Faraday,' he said quickly. 'Of course, all rich men get death threats from time to time. One would expect this sort of thing when Uncle Adrian was in the heyday of his career; when he was in the public eye. Not in his old age.'

He paused and looked at me searchingly with his steady grey eyes.

'I'm flattered you think I could help, Mr Faraday. I presume you can't take us into your confidence about the details.'

I blew a smoke-ring up toward the ceiling and watched it slowly dissolve into air. Like all the possible leads in this case so far.

'I wouldn't say that,' I said. 'I'll give you some more facts when you've come up with that list passing through your consciousness.'

Cameron laughed easily.

'You're a mind-reader, Mr Faraday. I was thinking about the laws of libel, to tell the truth. There have been a few people I could name. There was a man who acted as chauffeur for my uncle some years ago. I think he was sacked for theft. I can't exactly remember what he was called.'

'You needn't bother,' I said. 'I've eliminated him from my inquiries. But thanks for the lead, nevertheless.'

Cameron drummed on the desk-top restlessly. He glanced at a gold wristlet-watch clamped to his wrist.

'What about joining us for a cup of coffee, Mr Faraday? We usually have one about this time and it seems the morning for it.'

'Fine,' I said.

The dark-haired man swivelled his gaze over to the girl.

'Perhaps you'd ring for Chris, Ingeborg.'

The tall blonde got up with a supple movement.

'She stepped out, Joshua. I'll go see what I can rustle up.'

She gave me another brief exposure of the perfect teeth.

'I'd be obliged,' Cameron said.

He waited until the door had closed behind her.

'I'd trust Ingeborg with my life, Mr Faraday, but I'm glad she's gone for the moment.'

I looked at him sharply.

'Why?'

Cameron shrugged, leaning back in the padded chair, his grey eyes fixed up on the ceiling.

'Family skeletons, Mr Faraday,' he said. 'The old cliché, but true in our case. I'm not sure I'd want to parade them in front of everyone, even Ingeborg.'

He swivelled restlessly in the chair.

'There was something strange about the quarrel between Uncle Adrian and my mother. Something happened after my aunt's death. I never could understand, however much I tried.'

He broke off and looked at me fixedly.

'You haven't asked my uncle, I suppose?'

I shook my head.

'He hired me for a specific purpose. It hardly seemed appropriate.'

Cameron looked disappointed. He drummed on the desk-top again.

'No, of course not, Mr Faraday. I see that. You say he's had death-threats. You've seen the notes?'

I nodded.

'One only. He destroyed all the others. But there's no doubt about his concern and alarm.'

Cameron looked toward the door as though worried in case Ingeborg Svenson might reappear at any moment.

'Neither of us have been much help to the

other, Mr Faraday. But I'd like to help.'

'I'm sure, Mr Cameron,' I said. 'There was some mention of photographs. The threats were connected with them, it seems. Does that ring a bell?'

Cameron caught at his under-lip with very white teeth. He shook his head.

'I don't know what it could have been. Unless he'd been a naughty boy in the past. But it hardly seems likely.'

'That's what I thought,' I said. 'That mausoleum and the veneration in which he held his wife rules that out.'

There was a strange expression in Cameron's eyes.

'One odd thing about that mausoleum, Mr Faraday. It slipped my mind until now. It may be nothing . . .'

'Let's have it,' I said. 'Leads are a commodity I'm short of on this case.'

Cameron nodded.

'There's a vault underneath. It always used to intrigue me when I was a younger man. Maybe being an architect had something to do with it. I found some plans in the library one day. It's like a room, though I could never find the way into it. Underneath the sarcophagus of Mrs Zangwill, if I read the plans aright.'

'That's very interesting, Mr Cameron,' I said.

The dark-haired man inclined his head.

'I thought you'd find it so, Mr Faraday. It

174

may be nothing, of course. I gathered the old man intends to be buried there himself one day.'

Something flickered into my mind about the note Zangwill had showed me; about leaving the money in the mausoleum. If someone on the estate knew how to get into the room underneath he could retrieve the money in the dark. All he had to do was hide out in the vault for several days if necessary and slip out when it suited him. The more I thought about it the more I liked it.

Cameron looked dubious as his eyes searched my face.

'I don't know whether it's of any importance, Mr Faraday.'

'You've been a great help,' I said.

He smiled faintly.

'You haven't exactly come clean about this business.'

I stared at him through my cigarette-smoke.

'What makes you think that, Mr Cameron?'

'Instinct,' the dark-haired man said.

He leaned back at the desk and examined his fingernails. His strong head with the dark hair clustered thickly to the scalp made him look more like a Roman than ever. Not one of the Emperors, of course, but the decisive, clean-cut sort who might have been a vice-Consul. Though I didn't know why I was wasting time on these speculations this morning.

'You're maybe half-right,' I said. 'But I'm not entirely a free agent. A lot of money's been demanded from the old man, if that's what you mean.'

Cameron studied me from under half-lowered eyelids.

'I appreciate your frankness, Mr Faraday.'

'Like I said, nothing must go outside this room,' I told him. 'The old man knows I'm coming to see you, but he wouldn't like it if he knew how much I'd opened out.'

Cameron's face was creased with amusement now.

'I can imagine, Mr Faraday. I've been going over there for more than fifteen years. As fond as he is of me, he wouldn't like it at all. Like I said earlier, you have my word on the matter.'

He glanced up as the door behind us opened.

'Great, Ingeborg!' he said. 'Let's have some coffee and forget about all this business for a while, Mr Faraday.'

CHAPTER SEVENTEEN

1

It was almost lunch-time when I left Cameron's office. It was raining a treat again so I used one of the public phone-booths in the lobby and rang the office. Stella came on straight away and I gave her a resumé of the conversation I'd had.

'Useful,' she said.

'Useful enough,' I said. 'So far as it goes. That room underneath the mausoleum could be important.'

'We'll talk about it later,' Stella said. 'Something came up.'

'Old man Zangwill?' I said.

Stella shook her head. Don't ask me how I knew. I could see it even though a dozen miles separated us.

'A Mrs Hammond rang through about half-an-hour ago. She runs a place called the Santana Motel.'

'I know it,' I said. 'I stayed there once or twice.'

Stella ignored that.

'One of her guests went missing,' she said. 'He hasn't been back for several days. This morning she opened up his room. All his clothes and luggage were still there.'

'So?' I said.

'I haven't finished yet,' Stella said, little hints of impatience beginning to erode the edges of her syllables.

'She found a card in his room with our telephone number on it. Interested?'

'Interested,' I said.

'He'd obviously got it from the L.A. Directory,' Stella said. 'So she rang me. From the description she gave me it sounded like your little man.'

'Bertram?' I said. 'Remind me to raise your salary.'

'That'll be the day,' Stella said.

It was my turn to ignore her dialogue.

'I said you'd look on over there after lunch if I could contact you,' Stella said. 'I hope that was right.'

'Fine,' I said. 'I always like to have lunch first.'

Stella made a little rasping noise deep down in her throat that's meant to be sarcastic.

'I'll ring Mrs Hammond back to confirm the arrangement.'

'Great,' I said. 'And tell her not to contact the police for the moment.'

'She won't do that,' Stella said. 'They turned her place over once or twice before looking for hippies and suspected drug-pushers.'

'It's not that sort of set-up,' I said.

Stella chuckled.

'Apparently Mrs Hammond refused to contribute to the Policeman's Ball. She has decided views about the boys in blue.'

'She isn't the only one,' I said.

I thanked her and rang off. Then I got the Buick and tooled on over to Jinty's for a glass of lager and one of their blue-plate specials. Afterward, I drove to the Santana Motel. It wasn't far and though the traffic and the rain both were thickening up I made it in about half an hour.

The Santana had seen better days but it was still a fairly respectable, reasonably well-cared-for place, with gardens whose turf was mown regularly twice a week, when the sprinklers weren't working, and with hedges that still saw the shears frequently. Today the sprinklers weren't needed but a sad-looking individual in blue coveralls was painting the woodwork inside the glassed-in porch of the reception area as I came up.

I parked the Buick under a long blue awning and went in over Spanish tiles to a shadowy hallway. Mrs Hammond turned out to be a good-looking, fair-haired widow in her early forties, who wore blue jeans and a blue check shirt with style and grace. She looked me over hopefully as though long years of broken promises and passing-through clients had left her with undimmed optimism.

She was wearing rubber gloves and had been clipping and arranging roses in a big copper bowl on a table in the hall. Now she put the secateurs down and passed her gloved hand over her tumbling mass of natural blonde hair.

'I'm Faraday,' I said. 'You rang my office earlier.'

She smiled, showing good, strong teeth.

'Glad you got here so, early, Mr Faraday. I didn't know what to do. Mr Forrest hasn't been away at night at all ever since he got here.'

'How long has that been?' I said.

She focused her brown eyes into the far distance.

'Round about six weeks, Mr Faraday. Quiet, well-behaved man, always paid regularly.'

'Did he have an automobile?' I said.

She nodded, stripping the gloves off her lean, supple fingers.

'An Oldsmobile. He drove out in it one morning about three–four days ago. I don't remember exactly. But that was the last I saw of him.'

I nodded. I asked her to repeat the description she'd given Stella. From what she said it was Bertram all right.

'I'd like to see his room,' I said.

She crossed the hall with easy, athletic strides.

'I'll go get the key, Mr Faraday.'

She went in a door marked Office and came out again, a white raincoat thrown over her shoulders.

'It's only a few yards. Number 12.'

She stared at me as we went out the main entrance and down the concrete pathway fronting the white-painted blocks, each with its separate garage and entrance apron.

'Something's happened to him, hasn't it?'

I chose my answer with care.

'I don't think he'll be back again,' I said gently. 'If I were you I'd give it another week, just to make sure. You can store his stuff in the main block and re-let the apartment if you want. Then tell the police.'

Her eyes were wide and round. I paused as she stopped at the next bungalow and put the key in the main door.

'I'd appreciate it if you wouldn't tell them I was here. I came across Mr Forrest during confidential inquiries I'm making for a very rich client. It could be embarrassing all round.'

The Hammond number's face crinkled with puzzlement as she turned the key.

'I'm not quite sure I understand, Mr Faraday. But I'll be glad to do as you wish.'

She opened the door and stepped through. I followed.

'It's all above board,' I said.

'I'm sure it is,' she said gravely. 'I happen to know your secretary, Stella, through a tennis club we both belong to. She wouldn't be mixed up in anything shady.'

I grinned.

'Glad to hear you say so.'

The apartment we were in was the usual anonymous motel room though this was well decorated and kept. There were two open suitcases on racks at the end of the bed; a book and one or two items of clothing scattered about. A pair of pyjamas lay on the counterpane at the bedhead.

'If you want to look through his things I guess it'll be all right,' the blonde number said.

181

'I'll just go check the bathroom and garage in case he left anything that might be important.'

'Thanks,' I said.

I waited until she'd gone out. Then I went through Bertram's stuff quickly. I kept forgetting the name Zangwill's housekeeper had given him. Bassett. That was it. Presumably the proper name. I didn't expect to hit the jackpot but I was lucky this afternoon. There was a brown envelope at the bottom of the first case. I slit it open with my thumbnail. Mrs Hammond was running water in the bathroom now.

I felt something flat and metallic as I shook out the envelope. What I had was a large key, with a round metal tag. It had stamped on it the number: 184. Over the top was the name of a downtown bus depot. It seemed to burn a hole in my suit as I slipped it quietly into my pocket.

2

It was almost four-thirty by the time I got to the depot and the wind was competing with the rain to see which could make conditions the most unpleasant. There was a lot of long-haul stuff coming in and out and I had to go several blocks to the north before I found a place to park and got my ticket. Then I gum-shoed back down, my collar turned up against the driving rain. This had been a great case for pneumonia buffs. I guess my alcoholic intake had protected me from rheumatism.

There were a lot of people around in here but they were too busy groping for wet luggage, swearing and looking up their schedules to take any notice of me. Even so I felt exposed and in danger on this errand. The Smith-Wesson made a comforting pressure against my shoulder muscles as I got off the wet tarmac and into the brightly lit interior of the depot.

I kept my eyes peeled but it was almost impossible to take any precautions in a place like this. But I remembered Bertram and the suddenness with which the bungalow had gone up. There was a very real danger overhanging the people up at Zangwill's place and I didn't aim to make another statistic in the case. The key felt like it was burning a hole in my raincoat pocket.

It was lucky that Bertram had left a note of my number in his room. And lucky too that Mrs Hammond hadn't called in the police instead of ringing me. I had a feeling that things were beginning to turn. I skirted a glassed-in restaurant where sodden diners were watching Greyhounds reversing and making a lot of exhaust-smoke beyond the far glass wall. I was up in the locker area now, treading carefully down the aisles. There were only three people in here; an older woman; a younger, stamped out of the same pattern, who was obviously her daughter; and an obnoxious child who was banging on the metal locker doors and singing something inaudible in an off-key voice.

I resisted the temptation to beat him over the head with the Smith-Wesson as I went by; this case is making you brutal, Mike, I told myself. The mild joke lasted me all the way to the end of the aisle. I got out the key. I was hidden by an angle in the lockers from the three people farther back. They were obviously harmless but I tip-toed back and peeked around the corner just to make sure.

They were doing the same things as when I'd just passed; they'd gotten the key jammed in the lock and now the younger woman had it open and they were sorting out their luggage. I went back to the metal box I wanted. Locker No. 184 was just like the others but it looked like Pandora's Box to me at that moment. Especially as I'd been soaked to the bone for most of the case; when I wasn't being shot at, that is.

I wondered what I would do if the locker turned out to be empty. Go berserk, probably. I grinned, watching the rictus of my smile in a small mirror screwed to the far wall above the sets of grey steel boxes that marched down the aisle. I put the key in the lock and turned it. There was nothing in the locker but a big brown envelope, backed with cardboard.

I felt a pulse hammer in my temple as I picked it up. It was the right shape and size if it was what I hoped it would be. The bottom of the envelope was reinforced with thick card too; it was the type of thing photographers always used. I took it out the locker and closed the door, leaving the key in. I looked around but there was no one about.

The heavy throbbing of a diesel hammered the distance as one of the big buses lumbered out. I turned the envelope over. It bore Bertram's assumed name in big, spidery writing; that was obviously disguised too because I'd seen his name written on some of the photographs in the housekeeper's room up at Zangwill's and it was entirely different.

I shoved the envelope down inside my raincoat and got out the bus-depot fast. I walked several blocks back to the Buick and slid behind the wheel, locking the door behind me. I was plenty wet this time but for once I hadn't noticed. The rain drummed down on the windshield and streaked the glass. No-one could see me in here unless they came to within two feet of the driving door.

I opened the envelope with slightly quivering hands. There was another envelope and more cardboard inside. I don't know what I expected but it was entirely different to anything I could have imagined. I drew in my breath with a sharp, implosive sound as the dozen glossies came into view.

They were obviously copies of originals but they were clear and sharp enough to tell me most of the things I wanted to know. I shook the envelope but there were no negatives. I had a lot of the pieces now and a good idea of the whole set-up but there were still some things missing. I wouldn't find them by sitting around here. I gunned up the motor, reversed round, paid my parking fee and started making time across town.

CHAPTER EIGHTEEN

1

There was no-one in the lodge when I got up, to Zangwill's place and the wicket-gate was open, though the chains were across. It was almost dark by this time and I smelt disaster as I got out the Buick and put my size nines through the barriers and on to the old man's dangerous property. No alarm bells rang and no-one challenged me, but I remembered the Dobermann and I had the Smith-Wesson out before I'd gone two yards up the drive.

The image of the girl came again into my mind; either the most honest and sincere person I'd ever come across or a consummate actress. It could be either and like always I'd have to play everything by ear. I was alert for the slightest sound above the falling rain and my footsteps on the gravel seemed to rasp at the nerves. But I got up to the porch without being challenged. There were plenty of lights on in the house and I relaxed a little then.

Maybe the blond boy or Kempton was on patrol down by the lake and keeping the dog in check with one of those special whistles these people used. Maybe. I'd soon find out. I hit the bell and in a few seconds there were footsteps in the hall and light flooded down from the overhead lantern. Mrs Meakins was standing in the half-open doorway. She seemed astonished to see me.

'Good heavens, Mr Faraday. Is Miss Billington expecting you?'

'Something urgent came up. Something that won't wait. Is she at home?'

Mrs Meakins shut the door behind me with a ponderous crash.

'She's in her office, Mr Faraday. We're going to eat in about an hour. You want me to announce you?'

'I can find my way,' I said.

She saw me across the big hall and then went over toward her own sitting-room. My throat was dry as I rapped on the panels of the library door.

'Come in.'

It was Laura Billington's voice all right. I stood in the doorway, droplets of water still showering from my raincoat down on to the carpet.

'Hullo, Laura. Surprised to see me?'

'Mike!'

The girl's surprise was genuine enough. She got up from her desk and came over toward me, holding out her hands.

'You've found something?'

I nodded.

'Enough to split the case wide open.'

Her vivid violet eyes were curious but I couldn't see any guile in them. She led the way back toward the desk and the fire again.

'There's something funny here tonight,' I said. 'There was no-one in the lodge and the alarm isn't working.'

The girl had been standing with her back to me, like she was staring at the fire but now she turned round suddenly.

'Oh, surely not, Mike. Satan will be loose. And I expect Kempton will have been on patrol. He would have known you were on the grounds. I don't know how it works but the system is practically infallible.'

'Like it was yesterday,' I said. 'When that young guard and myself almost got killed.'

The girl flushed and came closer toward me. She reached up a slim, cool hand and gently touched my face. Despite the contradiction the touch seemed to change to fire. I'd be getting to like this if we did much of it. I moved away and damped down my enthusiasm.

'You didn't come up here to talk about the

alarm system.

I shook my head.

'I know why Mr Zangwill's being blackmailed and I have a fairly good idea who's involved. But there's still a lot of loose ends and I want you to help me.'

'I'll try,' the girl said.

There was shock in the eyes now.

'Is it bad?'

'Depends how you look at it,' I said. 'Manslaughter or murder, however the prosecution slanted it. Either way the old man's not going to like it.'

Laura Billington trembled and I moved closer to her but she was in control of herself again. She walked round the desk and dropped into her chair. I was aware now of stacks of neatly piled typescript and piles of photographs scattered about.

'What's all this?' I said. 'The old man making his will?'

The girl shook her head, her lips tightly compressed.

'That's not funny, Mike. Mr Zangwill is completing his autobiography in which he lays bare, for the first time, his sad life. It's taken a lot out of him.'

'I can imagine,' I said.

I went round the desk and leaned over the girl's shoulder. *THE FAR HORIZON* I read. *An Autobiographical Memoir by Adrian Zangwill.*

'Nice and flowery,' I said.

The girl shrugged.

'I thought it was pretty appropriate. He's always been far-seeing.'

I took up some of the typescript and riffled through it. One sentence on a page in the middle struck me and I studied it in silence. I read it aloud for the girl's benefit.

'Of all the mistakes and possibilities of one's life; of all the right and wrong decisions one might be called upon to make; there is a true path and wise indeed is the man who knows how to choose it. Now that I am nearing the far horizon of my own long life I see clearly, for the first time, that there is another horizon, beyond which one must eventually sink.'

I put the typescript back and stood in heavy silence for a moment, the weight of the whole case on my shoulders.

'Highly appropriate,' I said. 'You sure he's put everything in this book?'

The girl turned the pale oval of her face up to me.

'I don't understand you, Mike?'

'Take a look at these,' I said.

I got the sheaf of photos out the envelope and passed them over to her. She studied them with increasing agitation and then gave a choking cry.

'Pretty isn't it?' I said. 'And then the long, forty-year hypocrisy of that mausoleum out there.'

The girl was on her feet. A heavy tear rolled down her cheek and dropped to the desk.

'Where is he, by the way?' I said. 'In his room?'

The girl shook her head. Her voice was small and far away, like that of a child.

'He's gone down to the mausoleum. It's the anniversary of his wife's death next week and he had things to do.'

I looked at her as though I were seeing her for the first time.

'The mausoleum? Alone, at night?'

Laura Billington shook her head.

'He'll be quite safe. Kempton is back. He went with him.'

I stared at her, the cogs of my mind revolving uselessly. Then I turned, reaching for the Smith-Wesson.

'Take care of those photographs,' I told her. 'Ring the police and tell them to get out here. And stay put.'

'Where will you be?' she said. 'And what shall I tell the police?'

'Tell them to come armed,' I said. 'I may be outnumbered. But whatever you do, don't leave the house.'

I was back in the hall before she got to the phone. Then the front door was slamming behind me and I was alone with the darkness and the night as I pounded down the path toward the lake.

The wind was gusting and the rain was stinging my face. I seemed to have spent all my time on this case running through the grounds of old man Zangwill's estate; if not being shot at, then on fool's errands. I hoped I wouldn't be too late because I had a good idea of the plot-scenario now; it was only the fine detail and a few of the principal roles I had to fill in.

I transferred the Smith-Wesson to the side-pocket of my raincoat. I kept the safety on. I didn't want it going off in my pocket before I was ready. It was darker tonight but I could see the faint shape of the mausoleum growing in the blackness now, repeated in the steel-grey shimmer of the lake water at its foot.

I was about halfway around the lake when a blacker shadow launched itself from the shade of trees overhanging the path. But I'd already heard the click of claws on the gravel and though it gave me a jolt I was prepared. The eyes of Satan glowed like red coals in the dim light as he launched himself at me. There was just enough time for me to get to the Smith-Wesson, throw off the safety.

I got two slugs away as the dog was in mid-air. Its growling changed to a broken howl and then the big Dobermann was twisting over. It splashed heavily into the water and I heard it thrashing about in the reeds at the edge of the lake. I had no time to stop and I pounded on, perspiration mingling with the water that was streaming down my face. The dog had been the one thing I feared. It had been a lucky break.

The only problem now was whether my two shots had given the alarm. The noise of the wind and the rain wouldn't have been enough to cover them. They could have been heard all the way to L.A. and back. But if the room beneath the mausoleum was in use; as it might be on an occasion like this, then I might still take them by surprise.

Because if the old man aimed to be buried in a vault beneath the sarcophagus of his wife and he had gone down there tonight to supervise arrangements for his wife's anniversary he might take time out to review his own future; after all, he was over eighty.

I grinned to myself in the darkness. You're getting cynical, Faraday, I told myself. I stopped underneath the group of trees from which the dog had come. I reached for my spare clip in the Smith-Wesson harness and re-loaded. The Smith-Wesson .38 holds five and I might need all those shells before the evening was out.

I didn't really know what I expected to find but it was obvious to me now which way the situation had developed. My coming in had changed the whole ball-game. Bertram's intervention had only speeded things up. They'd tried to get us both with the jelly-bombs. The man by the mausoleum had done his best and almost succeeded. It could have been the same man in both instances, of course.

If I got lucky I'd know within the next couple of minutes. I moved off the path now and squelched across the grass. I made a wide circle, aiming to get in rear of the mausoleum. I wanted to know what was going on there before I barged in. The extra time wasn't that vital; the old man was in danger but they wouldn't kill him. Not until they'd got what they wanted. And they'd have to stage an accident; probably a drowning in the lake. Which would take a little time if they wanted it to look natural. And they'd sure as hell want that.

I was back in the grove of trees from which the triggerman had pinned me; nothing had changed except that now it was night instead of day. The weather was the same; I was the same; and the man I was looking for certainly hadn't changed. I aimed to get the jump on him tonight. I eased forward, holding the Smith-Wesson down in the folds of my raincoat, outside the pocket. I could see light now; it was coming from inside the big marble building.

It made a pale, leprous phosphorescence on the lower walls; I wondered why I hadn't seen it from the other side of the lake. Then I realized why. It was coming from so low down that it showed only some three or four feet up the inside walls of the mausoleum. The sarcophagus and the plinth masked most of it and the height the thing stood above the lake accounted for the rest. It was slightly wavering which made me figure that an oil lantern was probably being used.

I was so close now that I could see the light was coming from an oblong slit in the floor of the building, almost immediately behind the plinth. There was no-one around so I eased up the steps and into the mausoleum. The interior was in misty shadow except for the faint illumination from the stone stairway that went down at a shallow angle. I could see that a big stone slab had been hauled aside.

I kept the Smith-Wesson up and went over; the light was coming from a vault chamber a long way below. There were wet foot-prints on the stone steps and a murmur of voices. I gum-shoed slowly down, my heart beating in heavy, muted thumps. It was too far to make out the dialogue for the moment.

The staircase levelled out on a sort of stone landing and there was a broad stone lintel that led to a second set of shallow steps. It was dark here and I paused to get my bearings. That was when I heard a boot scrape on the upper flight of steps behind me. I had no time to turn. I was at the right-hand side of the door and only the left part of my body was silhouetted against the light.

I put my right hand up, found a broad ledge above the door; in the darkness I just had time to balance the Smith-Wesson on it. The safety was already off. I put my hand back to my side and started to turn. I froze as something blunt dug into my spine.

'Go on down, Faraday,' a hard, familiar voice said. 'You'll be among friends.'

CHAPTER NINETEEN

1

I put my hands above my head, like the man said. Apparently he hadn't noticed anything. He ran a heavy hand over me from behind. We were halfway down the steps now.

'What happened to your piece?' he said suspiciously.

'I fell in with your dog back there,' I said. 'I took him out but the firearm ended up in the lake.'

He sucked at his teeth with an irritating noise in the stillness.

'Pity about Satan,' he said. 'You'll be joining him before the evening's out. You'll be sorry the dog didn't finish you. He would have been quicker and kinder about it.'

'I can imagine,' I said.

I felt a heavy blow then and fell forward down the remaining steps. I must have passed out for a few seconds and when I came around I tasted blood and had difficulty in focusing. Kempton stood above me, a hard, angry figure, still in the same slicker and wideawake hat he was wearing the first time I'd seen him. The two people standing by the central plinth in the low vault chamber looked up in alarm. The third was old man Zangwill; he knelt by the plinth and there was blood on the dusty white hair but a proud and indomitable look in his eyes.

'I'm sorry I got you involved in this, Mr Faraday,' he said.

'Think nothing of it,' I told him.

Kempton moved forward, his boot raised, but the dark-haired man standing near the oil lamp shifted over to stop him.

'That will do,' he said sharply.

He looked pale as though this wasn't really his scene.

'Murder always does run in families, doesn't it?' I said.

Joshua Cameron inclined his Roman head regretfully.

'It's a sad fact of life, Mr Faraday. But you'd better ask Mr Zangwill about that. He swindled me out of my rightful heritage. My mother got nothing from her sister's will.'

'She didn't need anything,' I said. 'She was

already rich. What did you do, gamble it away?'

Cameron shook his head impatiently.

'It's all tied up in trusts, Mr Faraday. I get to use some of the interest. Which wasn't enough to keep my business from failing.'

I got up on to one knee and steadied myself against the wall. A trickle of blood ran down into my eyes. I guess I must have slammed up against one of the three central vault pillars when Kempton knocked me down the steps. He went to stand against the wall and lit a cigarette. The big automatic in his hand was centred rock-steady on my gut.

'We all have our problems,' I said.

I looked at the girl. Ingeborg Svenson's face was white and strained but she still looked beautiful and deadly in a black and white zebra-striped raincoat. The little nickel-plated revolver in her right hand trembled slightly as she kept it on the kneeling figure of the old man resting against the plinth. On top of it lay an envelope, some documents and an open cheque-book. The pen had fallen from Zangwill's fingers to the floor. Cameron bent to pick it up and put it back near the old man's motionless hand.

'I got most of the story,' I said. 'Will you tell it or shall I?'

The girl shrugged.

'It hardly matters now, Mr Faraday. Earlier, you were becoming quite a nuisance. After tonight it's of no consequence.'

198

I smiled at her, getting cautiously to my feet. A trip-hammer was at work now, somewhere in the back of my skull.

'Even if you persuade Mr Zangwill to sign that cheque, do you think it will be easy collecting half a million dollars from the bank? They'll want verification, proper authorization. And they're bound to check with the estate.'

Kempton's eyes were still hard and angry but he seemed more at ease now. The barrel of his piece had dropped a couple of inches or so and was aimed at my knees.

'You let us worry about that, Faraday,' he said softly.

'Sure,' I said.

I moved over to stand beside one of the pillars. Kempton's gun shifted across to remain trained on me.

'It was a little confusing at first,' I said. 'It took me some while to catch on. It was obviously an inside job but I fixed on the wrong man initially. I thought it was Bassett, the chauffeur, especially when he approached me with an identical offer to yours.'

None of the people in the vault said anything; old man Zangwill, still wearing the same brown suit with the plus fours looked like something out of a thirties melodrama. His eyes had a pleading look as he stared at me.

'Nothing made sense; all the business of the intruders and the shots; particularly leaving

199

the money in the niche of the mausoleum above. It was all a big act to confuse and frighten Miss Billington and Mr Zangwill here.'

Joshua Cameron looked every inch the clean-cut executive as he listened politely.

'You're doing fine, Faraday,' he said, with an encouraging grin.

My nerves were steadying up now and the pounding in my skull had receded.

'What would you have done if the money had been left here? Hidden in the vault? Have come out for the money after dark and then disappeared?'

The girl gave me an angry glance.

'We had it all worked out, Mr Faraday. It would have been fine.'

I turned to Kempton.

'You exchanged shots with yourself the night the intruder was supposed to have got in. You fired four into the air and then re-loaded with two. You knew the alarm system inside out and people only got into the grounds when it was your night off. So you had to be sparing with those effects. How did you fix the fake attack on the girl?'

Kempton's lazy smile widened another couple of millimetres.

'That was just to add a little colour. Mr Cameron had come to see me in the lodge that afternoon. When the girl came we talked for a while. Mr Cameron changed into his outfit and hid in the car to scare her and give a little authority to the chaos I was spreading about.'

Cameron gave me a grudging smile.

'You haven't done so badly, Mr Faraday. If it hadn't been for Bassett you'd never have gotten on to us.'

I nodded.

'Maybe. He was a member of your team originally. But he went into business for himself. He took copies of those photographs. That's why he didn't have the negatives. He was a little more subtle than you were. He wanted to do a deal with Mr Zangwill through me for the same amount you were after.'

I turned back to the big security guard.

'You weren't quite as careful as you might have been. I noticed your veteran's tie. You had ex-marine written all over you. You followed me when I went out to that bungalow. You were good at keeping out of sight. You figured it would be an excellent idea to take us both out.'

Kempton shrugged, his eyes flickering with malice.

'I felt sure I'd gotten you both. You're pretty durable.'

'It was your big mistake,' I said. 'It pinpointed you. Those things were a feature of the jungle war in Vietnam. You might just as well have had your name on them.'

Kempton smiled a lazy smile.

'It's all academic now, Faraday.'

'Perhaps,' I said. 'Then I had a break. The woman who owns the motel where Bassett was holed out rang me. She'd found a piece of paper in his room with my number on it. I went out there and found the key to a locker at a downtown bus-depot where he'd stashed the photo-copies.'

I turned back to the kneeling figure of the old man.

'Which brings me back to you, Mr Zangwill. Why did you kill your wife?'

2

The old man made a choking noise and his face turned a nasty mottled colour. The girl got to him, lowered him to the floor where he sat with his back to the plinth, fighting for breath. I looked slowly round the vault. Despite the girl's automatic and the big pistol Kempton held on me there seemed more polite interest among the tight triangle of three people than menace.

'I can appreciate your feelings,' I told Cameron.

The irony seemed lost on the young architect. He gave me a slightly mocking bow.

'That's very good of you, Mr Faraday. Let's see how good you are. How do you read the situation?

Kempton interrupted, impatience in his

voice. He glanced significantly at his watch.

'Let's get on with it.'

Cameron shook his head.

'We'll hear him out, Kempton. It's amusing. And we've got all night if necessary. The girl won't come out here after what's happened.'

He leaned back against the pillar, his eyes flickering from the crushed figure of the old man and then on to me.

'We'll give you ten minutes, Mr Faraday. Then, if Mr Zangwill won't co-operate we'll take a little trip out to the lake.'

'I don't think so,' I said. 'That would spoil your plans.'

Kempton showed his teeth briefly.

'Don't bank on our patience, Faraday.'

'I'll get to the meat, then,' I said.

I turned back to Cameron.

'Your mother was a very fine photographer. One of the best of her class from what I've seen back at the house. She was out photographing the grounds that day in 1939 when her sister Gloria died. She was concentrating on landscapes. Maybe she didn't know what she'd got there. But in any case the pictures were put to the back of her mind by the accident that happened up here.'

I looked reflectively at the dejected old man lying by the plinth and I felt a sudden stab of pity.

'I don't know why you did it, Mr Zangwill. But you had a quarrel that day. You knocked her to the ground. It's my guess it was a sudden fit of temper. Your business empire was collapsing. Your wife had millions in her own right. You asked her for a loan to tide you over. She refused and you struck her. Correct so far?'

Zangwill nodded his white head mutely.

'You were genuinely appalled and horrified when you found she was dead. But you were nothing if not resourceful. You were a man of formidable strength. You broke the horse's girth yourself and sent it back riderless to give the alarm. Then, after a decent interval you presented yourself at the house in time to lead the search party which found the body.'

I was getting tired and thirsty with all this talking; the four other people in the vault listened politely like we were coming to the climax of some play in which they felt very little interest. I was beginning to feel that way myself.

'You saved your business empire,' I told Zangwill. 'But you lost your own soul. You were consumed by guilt and you'd ruined your own life. You built this tomb out here by way of expiation.'

There was a thunderous silence in the vault now like an electrical storm was about to burst overhead. I looked at Cameron.

'Later on, your mother developed the pictures she'd taken that fatal afternoon. She made enlargements of detail and found she had a murder scene right in the middle of her lens. A number of shots showing Zangwill striking the blow; kneeling over his wife on the ground; and breaking the horse's girth. She had enough on her brother-in-law to indict him for manslaughter and concealment of a crime. Instead, she kept silent all those years. She cut her brother-in-law out of her life, though she could hardly explain the reason why. She discouraged you from coming here when you were a child. And she kept the pictures locked away in a drawer.'

I glanced at Zangwill. He seemed like a figure carved in stone himself as he leaned back against the plinth.

'That was the situation that obtained for nearly forty years,' I told Cameron. 'Until your mother died about a year ago. You were going through her things a while back and found the photographs. You decided to put the bite on your uncle. You found yourself some allies in Kempton and the disgruntled chauffeur and the melodrama was under way.'

I went over and stood looking down at the old man slumped on the floor.

'I guessed there was something phoney about the situation but I couldn't figure what. You destroyed the first notes in the blackmail series because you didn't dare let anyone see them. They spelled out too specifically the situation. Which would have let you in for a charge of manslaughter or possibly even third degree murder.'

The old man sat on as though he were deaf and dumb.

'Even then you wouldn't give up without a fight. You stalled for as long as possible before calling me in. You knew that if you paid, these people wouldn't stop at half a million dollars.'

The old man spoke for the first time, raising his eyes from the floor.

'That's right, Mr Faraday. I'm sorry you found out the truth about me. It's not very savoury. But what are you going to do about these people?'

I held out my hands wide.

'Very little I can do, Mr Zangwill. I guess you'd do better to sign that cheque.'

I could sense rather than see the surprise on the faces of the girl and the other two men.

'That's the first sensible thing you've said since you dropped in,' Cameron said.

The old man raised his eyes defiantly to mine.

'Just sign,' I said gently.

I was half-turned toward the others and I drooped my right eyelid over my eye. The old man was smart. He's seen what I was after right away. He made a great act of it. He gave a heavy sigh, his shoulders sagging.

'If you say so, Mr Faraday. If there's no other way out of it.'

I shook my head.

'We have no choice, Mr Zangwill. Not if we

want to walk out of here.'

Zangwill dragged himself to a kneeling position. He looked an incredible sight in the yellow light of the oil lamp. He reached out for the pen and the chequebook and started writing with a sharp scratching noise that echoed round the vault and began to scald the nerves.

'So your mother was rich but you couldn't touch her money,' I said.

Cameron nodded.

'That's right, Mr Faraday. And business was going downhill. I have very expensive tastes. And a very expensive girl-friend.'

'Why did you tell me about this vault when I visited your office?' I said.

Cameron shrugged.

'It added to my plausibility, Mr Faraday. And the mystery.'

Cameron and the blonde girl held each other's smiling gaze. I shook my head, looking at Kempton who stood, menacing and apart, at the vault entrance.

'What a family. I don't know which of you has been the more self-destructive.'

Cameron took a step toward me, little patches of red standing out on his cheeks.

'It's not for you to judge us, Mr Faraday.'

'Maybe not,' I said.

I waited until Zangwill had finished writing the cheque and had torn it from the book. The girl leaned over and took it with trembling fingers.

'This is where we take a little walk,' Cameron said.

He couldn't keep the triumph out of his voice. He took the cheque from the girl like it was red-hot and put it in his wallet with unsteady fingers.

'We follow the routine we agreed,' he said. 'We want the letter from my uncle too but we can't do all that here. We fix Faraday first.'

'I'm in no hurry,' I said.

Kempton gave a low, lazy smile. The girl was over helping the old man. Cameron was stooping, lifting Zangwill by his left arm. Kempton motioned with the pistol.

'Just take it nice and easy, Faraday, or you get it here.'

'I'll take it easy,' I said.

'Put your hands up.'

I turned around and did like he said. This was getting better all the time. If things turned out the way I wanted he'd just written himself off. And I knew I had to take him out if I was going to stay alive myself. I walked up the steps, keeping my hands high. That was when I remembered a major difficulty. Coming in, I'd naturally been facing the other way. Going out I'd have to get to the gun with my left. And because I'm right-handed that might be tricky.

I was up near the top of the flight now. I could hear Kempton's boots scraping behind me. It was dark here. Someone started turning the lamp down. That was when the groping fingers of my left hand found the Smith-Wesson on the sill above the door. I kicked out backward with all my strength.

CHAPTER TWENTY

1

There was a dull crack as my shoe connected with Kempton's knee-cap. He gave a groan of pain. Then I had the Smith-Wesson in both hands and whirled round while his own barrel was in the air. He was off-balance and going down when I blew him away but this was no time for niceties. The explosion of the two shells seemed to take the top of my head off in the confined space.

Kempton's face looked sick and stupid. Two big holes rimmed with blood were punched into his chest. All this I saw in the two split-seconds that the muzzle-flashes took to light up the vault. Then Kempton was hurled backward down the steps. He crashed into Cameron and the two went over in a welter of arms and legs.

There were yells and cries of pain. I went down the steps, slipped and cannoned into the side wall. Perhaps it was just as well because in the mood I was in I might have just gone on pumping shells until the chambers were empty. Which is always a mistake. I saw old man Zangwill and the girl in the dim light from the oil lamp, which had been turned halfway down. There was a thunderous explosion and dust-chips rained into my face as a hole was gouged into one of the big dressed stones composing the wall.

I dived away, landed badly but I was in the darkness behind one of the pillars. The firing had been coming from Cameron. I guessed he would have been armed but I didn't think he would have reacted so quickly. I rolled away as another shot blammed out. The slug went whining round the close confines of the square vaulted chamber. I was hugging the floor now, my eye round the bottom of the pillar. I couldn't see what the girl or Zangwill were doing. He'd sunk back on to his haunches and Ingeborg had been standing over him with the pistol when last I'd seen them.

I could have aimed for the oil lamp, of course. With that out there would have been complete darkness. But it was also another and pretty fool-proof way of committing suicide down here. And I didn't aim to get killed by a ricochet in the dark. It was quiet for the moment so I took the opportunity to re-load. That meant I still had five.

I was confident I could take Cameron out unless he had extraordinary luck. I didn't count the girl. Her pistol was just a toy and

210

she'd have to be working at very close range to do any real damage. And I didn't aim to let her get close. Kempton was dead long ago, of course. I'd made sure of that. He was the only pro among these people and he'd been at the top of my list.

At the moment light began to grow in the vault. I had a quick look round the pillar. I was just in time to see the girl's fingers turning up the lamp. I grinned. That would be equally useful to me. It was good light for shooting now. And I was a better shot than anyone here.

I couldn't see anybody except Zangwill. The old man was lying crumpled and broken by the plinth like he didn't care what happened to him. He probably didn't come to that. The girl and Cameron were the other side of the plinth, back in deep shadow. I pulled my feet in, got close up to the pillar to give them as small a target as possible.

A quavering voice sounded in the heavy silence. It was Cameron's.

'Can we deal, Faraday?'

I shook my head.

'No deals.'

'What do you propose, then. It's two against one.'

'It still doesn't add up to very much opposition,' I said. 'I'm a pro, remember.'

Cameron's voice sounded incredulous.

'You mean to say we should simply give up

half a million, hand you our guns and walk out of here prisoners?'

I grinned.

'Talk sense, Cameron. You never had half a million. You'll never have half a million. Give yourself a break. Laura Billington rang the police before I came down. They'll be here any minute.'

I got in behind the pillar. Cameron fired a fusillade of shots. I figure the whole chamber. I was half-deafened and the slugs whined like crazy about the stone walls. He was endangering himself more than anyone else. But I guess he had to get it out of his system. I looked round the pillar.

He was kneeling the other side of the plinth re-loading. I took careful aim and got him in the shoulder. There was surprise in his eyes as the slug punched him away, scarlet spreading on the front of his suit. The girl screamed. I was on my feet as she came round the plinth with the pistol. That was when old man Zangwill made his contribution. The blonde girl screamed again as her wrist cracked. He bent her backward and the pistol tinkled to the stone floor.

I had his own wrist as he tried to bring the weapon to his head.

'Not this time, Mr Zangwill,' I said. 'You've paid for whatever you've done with forty years of remorse. Just try trusting people.'

The film of madness cleared from his eyes

as he stared at me. The girl made a moaning noise and went to cradle Cameron's head.

'What do you mean, Mr Faraday'

'That you've still got a lot to live for, Mr Zangwill, even at your age. Go finish that book of yours. *The Far Horizon*, isn't it? Besides, Miss Billington believes in you.'

The old man eased himself to his feet until he towered over me kneeling on the floor.

'What about those photographs? The murder charge?'

'It's a long time ago,' I said. 'You've suffered a lot. I'm sure the courts will be lenient with an old man.'

Zangwill drew himself up with a sort of crushed nobility on his face.

'Maybe you're right, Mr Faraday. I'll give it a try.'

There were heavy footsteps then and suddenly the vault was filled with hard-faced men in blue uniforms, brandishing revolvers. I got up slowly, feeling old and passé and beat-up. Like always the law had come when it was all over.

2

A thin rain tapped at the windows. Stella sat with her head cupped in her hands and looked at me reflectively.

'So it all came right in the end?' she said.

'I wouldn't have said exactly that,' I told her. 'Kempton got dead; the chauffeur got dead; I got considerably beat-up; the old man and the girl had six months of misery; Cameron and his girl are going down for quite a few years.'

Stella smiled faintly.

'You know I didn't mean that, Mike.'

I shrugged, turning my eyes up to the cracks in the ceiling.

'You mean about Zangwill. The judge held an al fresco hearing in camera.'

Stella raised her eyebrows.

'So we got education this morning,' she said.

I ignored that.

'Like I said, they were easy on him. A suspended sentence and nothing gets out to the public. It's something to do with tempering justice with mercy.'

I stared at the rain streaking the window panes.

'That was his atonement,' I told Stella. 'To be buried below his wife.'

'Like the old Crusaders had a dog at their feet,' Stella said. 'What a world.'

She got up and went over to the alcove. She bustled about with cups and saucers and the percolator.

'What I can't understand is Cameron and the girl keeping quiet,' she said.

I shrugged.

'Family feeling. They'll go down for threats and extortion. They decided too that the old man had gone through enough. There'll be sufficient evidence for the D.A. in the death-threat note, my testimony and that of Zangwill.'

I sighed and looked out at the misty boulevard.

'I'll be lucky not to be bounced off my licence.'

Stella put her head round the corner of the glassed-in alcove and smiled. I could have sat there and watched it all day.

'You never quite do that, Mike,' she said. 'Zangwill's deposition alone will be enough to get you off the hook.'

She came and stood near me.

'What did they hope to achieve with that cheque, Mike? It wouldn't have been legal, being obtained under duress.'

I shook my head.

'There was a little more to it than that. My guess is they would have taken me out first and buried me on the estate in some place no-one would ever have found me. They would have taken the old man down to the lodge and got him to sign a typed letter authenticating the cheque and giving as his reason the situation that his sister-in-law and nephew never benefited from his wife's vast estate at her death.'

Stella looked at me sombrely.

'The dates would have been the important factors,' I said. 'The old man would have been found drowned in the lake the next day. The cheque and letter would have had to be proved in court eventually but I don't think there's any doubt Cameron would have got his money in the end.'

I stared up at the cracks in the ceiling.

'Cameron made one mistake when I interviewed him. He knew his mother was a great photographer. Yet when I mentioned photography he was careful not to react. That was one thing he dare not risk.'

I lit a cigarette and watched the blue smoke wavering upward.

'Human nature's a funny thing,' I said. 'Cameron, the girl and Kempton were quite ready to kill the old man for what they wanted. But as soon as they knew the money was lost for ever they decided to spare the uncle's feelings. Cameron and Ingeborg, I mean. The nephew would have got all the money at his uncle's death, anyway.'

I ran my finger across my chin.

'Maybe they'll go find an old people's home, marry and live happily ever after when they get out.'

Stella came over and stood looking down at me.

'You'll never understand human nature, Mike,' she said softly. 'Maybe they will at that.'

I waited until she put the steaming coffee cup down on my blotter.

'I should have got on to Kempton earlier,' I

said. 'But all these stories about shootings around the estate put me off. Plus the stuff with the blond boy.'

I looked into Stella's calm, very blue eyes. I focused up on my coffee cup again.

'Kempton was very careful not to explain why the alarms had failed when describing the first raid on the grounds,' I said. 'They hadn't been triggered, of course, because he was firing all the shots himself from inside.'

Stella came and sat down in the client's chair with her own cup.

'What about those photographs, Mike?'

'The judge ordered they should be destroyed, along with the negatives,' I said. 'I was present with Sheriff's Office staff when the ceremony took place.'

Stella shivered like it had grown cold in here.

'How did Cameron and the chauffeur, Bassett, and Kempton get tied up in the first place?'

'Nothing to it,' I said.

I picked up my coffee cup. Like always, the brew tasted great.

'Cameron had been going out there for years. It was one of those schemes which gradually crystallized over a long period. It might have worked too if Bassett hadn't decided to go into business for himself.'

Stella put down her cup with a clinking in the silence.

'You suspected Laura Billington at one stage,' she said.

'You put that thought into my head,' I said. 'They were quite clever about it. Those letters could have been posted by anyone. And they'd have had a ready-made scapegoat in case of need.'

'She rang in earlier today,' Stella said, like it was an afterthought. 'The old man's invited us up for dinner tomorrow night. He probably wants to present you with one of his zinc-mines.'

I grinned.

'His first cheque was big enough.'

Stella looked across to the window. Incredibly, light was growing through the clouds.

'The sun's breaking through. It will soon be spring.'

She got up and came to sit on the edge of my desk, waiting for me to finish my first cup.

'Why wouldn't Zangwill's wife lend him money to save his businesses in 1939, Mike?'

'She hated his industrial interests,' I said. 'She never saw him, he was so busy. So she refused. It was her way of bringing him to his senses.'

'But it destroyed two lives instead,' Stella said softly.

'That's the way it goes sometimes,' I said.

The phone buzzed just then. Stella cupped the receiver, glanced at me, the corners of her

218

mouth turned down.

'Sounds like another stake-out job, Mike.'

I looked over toward the window, where the strengthening light was dispersing the rainclouds.

'At least it will be fine for it,' I said.